RISING TIDE

A RICK AND JOJO ADVENTURE

ARMAND ROSAMILIA, TOM DUFFY

RYMFIRE BOOKS

Copyright © 2025 by Armand Rosamilia, Tom Duffy

All rights reserved.

No portion of this book may be reproduced in any form without written permission from the publisher or author, except as permitted by U.S. copyright law.

ARMAND'S MAILING LIST

Are you a fan of suspense thrillers?

Join Armand Rosamilia's mailing list
Lots of exclusive content, news about upcoming thriller books,
appearances and more.
Sign up now and get a free story, too!
https://armandrosamilia.com

Contents

1. ONE — 1
2. TWO — 6
3. THREE — 11
4. FOUR — 16
5. FIVE — 21
6. SIX — 26
7. SEVEN — 31
8. EIGHT — 36
9. NINE — 41
10. TEN — 46
11. ELEVEN — 51
12. TWELVE — 56
13. THIRTEEN — 61
14. FOURTEEN — 67
15. FIFTEEN — 72
16. SIXTEEN — 78

17. SEVENTEEN 83
18. EIGHTEEN 88
19. NINETEEN 94
20. TWENTY 99
21. TWENTY-ONE 105
22. TWENTY-TWO 110
23. TWENTY-THREE 115
24. TWENTY-FOUR 121
25. TWENTY-FIVE 127
26. TWENTY-SIX 132
27. TWENTY-SEVEN 138
28. TWENTY-EIGHT 143
29. TWENTY-NINE 148
30. THIRTY 153
31. THIRTY-ONE 158
32. THIRTY-TWO 163
33. THIRTY-THREE 169
34. THIRTY-FOUR 174
35. THIRTY-FIVE 179
36. THIRTY-SIX 184
37. THIRTY-SEVEN 189
38. THIRTY-EIGHT 194

39.	THIRTY-NINE	200
40.	FORTY	205
41.	FORTY-ONE	210
42.	FORTY-TWO	215
43.	FORTY-THREE	220
44.	FORTY-FOUR	225
45.	FORTY-FIVE	230
46.	FORTY-SIX	235
47.	FORTY-SEVEN	240
48.	FORTY-EIGHT	246
49.	FORTY-NINE	251
50.	FIFTY	257
About the Author		262
About the Author		263

ONE

We don't know where the treasure is, JoJo thought as she sat outside back at Cuba's place.

Sure, they found a wreck but that's it. And wrecks in any ocean are common enough, especially close to the shore.

Since she hadn't been talking to Rick much, JoJo spent the last couple weeks reading up on shipwrecks. She didn't know if it would help in this situation, but the books were helpful in terms of letting her know how boats would get scuttled on reefs coming in and how they age and rot under water.

Science wasn't her strong suit, but JoJo figured any little thing she could learn would, at the least, be interesting and could possibly help with their situation.

She had been depressed that the first dive didn't immediately come up with some money. She also didn't particularly enjoy being stuck in a house with Cuba. Granted, he wasn't bad to look at, but JoJo felt like she was in a prison.

Rick didn't seem to care. He looked like he didn't have a feeling one way or the other. JoJo didn't know if it was because they had no choice or because he was thinking about other things. His addiction.

JoJo looked around her and wondered if she had made the right choice leaving the states for Mexico. It was a beautiful country, but there were too many things to watch out for. Dangerous things. It wasn't just the animals that could kill you. The people would kill you. The cartel was everywhere.

Her head moved to the sound of someone coming around the corner. Another guard with a gun. She nodded at him. The man didn't respond and walked back around the house.

The door behind her slid open. JoJo sighed. She'd been through this before and knew who was going to sit next to her.

Rick sat and put an arm around her. JoJo flinched and didn't like that reaction.

They'd been together for so long and she knew that she loved him, but there was just something she couldn't get over. The drugs being in her face was too much.

"How are you?" Rick asked.

"Why are you asking me that?"

"I just want to make sure you're doing okay."

JoJo took a deep breath and looked into the jungle.

"You've said that over and over again. I told you I need time. Why do you keep pressuring me?"

"I'm not pressuring you. I just want to make sure we're good. I fucked up. I know that. But I'm owning up to it."

"No, Rick. We're not good. I went into this life with you knowing you had a past. But you were good. You were good for a long time. Then you pull out a balloon. And I know it was to help the kid, but you shouldn't have had it on you to begin with."

"Is it Cuba?"

"Are you not listening to me? I never brought him up. It's you and you're slipping backwards. I know you haven't done anything, but you've been thinking about it. I don't know how to deal with this. I can't be with you in the past. Addiction doesn't just affect you. It hurts everyone around you, and right now I'm the only person around you."

JoJo didn't know what to say. She didn't want to tell Rick how she felt. At the same time, JoJo needed to be honest with him.

"It wasn't supposed to be this hard," she said.

"What?"

"Coming down here. Sure, we were running away from stuff, but we were also supposed to be running toward something. And for a little while it was great. But it feels like we're not moving, in any direction. It's like winning the lotto, blowing through it all, and having to go back to that same shitty job you quit."

"I know it's been a lot of work, but we're great at it together. And this job. This is the key to that beach house with umbrella drinks and mid-afternoon naps."

JoJo smirked and looked at the sky.

"You know who you sound like? Always promising there's a big score around the corner. Look where that got him."

"So what do you want to do? You want to hang it up? Retire? Buy a tiki bar or something and go legit? I'm telling you, I'm done with the drug shit. I have been for a while. Sure I may have started a slide, but I caught myself before I couldn't stop."

JoJo kissed Rick on the edge of his lips. She couldn't see the future, but knew that there was a chance she may not want Rick in it. At least maybe not until she can get things straightened out on her end. Who was she kidding? Neither of them had their shit together. It's just JoJo didn't feel the phantom prick of a needle when she was spiraling.

"We do this job. Somehow, I don't know how at this point, we get this treasure out, avoid being killed by Cuba or the cartel, or that little shit kid. Then we go. Somewhere new and somewhere where we can settle."

"And if the treasure is bullshit?"

"Well, that wouldn't be too much different than most of our experiences in the past. Everybody moves on, the whole thing is a giant waste of time, and nothing much changes."

"And with us?" Rick asked.

"One thing at a time."

Cuba stepped outside, interrupting a conversation JoJo didn't want to continue anyway.

"Got news on that street kid. Gonna be fine. One of my guy's said he's already out. Tough little shit."

"You got part of that right," JoJo said. She stood up and wiped some pool water off her legs, then paused. "What?" She noticed the look on Cuba's face.

"That guy? The one chasing and shooting at everyone?"

"Raul," JoJo said.

"Yeah. Dead on the beach. Plain daylight and nobody saw a thing, even though there were plenty of people around."

"The only person–"

"Maria."

"But why?"

"You might want to sit back down again. Then you might want to grab a shit ton of body armor. The little shit is her kid. I don't think she's going to be very happy you almost got him killed.

TWO

Maria had been expecting this meeting for days but she was still trying not to shake. She reached to pick up her glass of tequila but stopped herself.

The door to the meeting room opened and in walked The Wolf.

He'd gotten heavier in the past year or so, since Maria had last seen him. More fat around the middle. His face was droopy and his eyes bloodshot and sunken.

"Maria, darling," The Wolf said and sat across from her.

Three of his men, all well-armed, entered and took up positions in the corners, equidistant.

Maria knew one of the men had been placed strategically behind her, in her blindspot. If this meeting went south she knew she wouldn't even know she had been killed.

"Hello, " Maria said and forced a smile. She knew The Wolf, the head of the Orenato Cartel, wasn't currently in Mexico City for the tequila, for the football or for the views.

He's here because they found Raul, Maria thought.

When word had come down to her that The Wolf was flying from Colombia, the stronghold of the cartel, to see her personally, she'd at first wanted to flee the country.

Maria knew there wasn't a corner of the world she could hide, though. Better to take her lumps and see what he had planned.

Even though the Orenato Cartel had no obvious power with the Sinaloa Cartel, Maria knew there was more to it than a simple hierarchy. Without the Orenato family there would be no drugs through Mexico, no narco subs on the coastlines and no human trafficking coming through South and Central America.

"Raul is dead," The Wolf said. His eyes bore into Maria. No emotion. She thought he had shark's eyes. Dead.

"Yes, I heard that, too. My condolences." Maria didn't know what else to say, and she wasn't going to divulge any information about Raul unless directly confronted with it. She also knew it would take The Wolf and his men having to torture her in order to eventually find out Maria had killed Raul herself.

The Wolf shook his head. "Do you have any idea why Raul was in Punta Prieta, when he clearly enjoyed his home here in Mexico City? It seems like a long way out of his way, if you ask me."

"And now you're asking me," Maria said and shrugged. "I cannot tell you what Raul was thinking, because I never asked him why he was in Punta Prieta. Perhaps he liked being on the coast, near the ocean."

"Not likely," The Wolf said. "Raul would never leave the safety of Mexico City without a reason, and we both know that reason was always usually money."

Maria shrugged, trying not to get too excited. She hoped this was as it seemed, nothing more than a fishing expedition from The Wolf to find out what had happened to Raul.

He knew nothing about the man's death other than his body had been found, which she knew would eventually happen.

"I did not know Raul all that well," Marisa said. "Yes, we worked together on and off for a number of years, and he was a valuable asset whenever I was in a certain part of Mexico, but... he was distant, as you know Raul could be."

She didn't want to give any more information than she needed to give to this man, who could raise his fist and her life would end.

Maria didn't fear any man... but The Wolf was close enough he unnerved her. This man had absolute power over most, if not all, cartels in the world. It was said the Russian mafia had a million dollar bounty on his head.

"It seems like you spent quite a bit of time together while in that little town," The Wolf said and sat back in his chair. "In fact, it is a special place for you, no?"

Maria nodded. "I was born there."

"And you still have family there," The Wolf said.

Maria knew enough to read between the lines. He might know about Ignacio. He would definitely know about her sister and cousins who lived in Punta Prieta.

"I do," Maria said simply.

"Raul was killed by someone and I need to know who did this and why they did it. I want you to figure this out..." The Wolf grinned. "Unless you have other, more important things to do right now."

"Nothing would be more important than finding out what happened to Raul," Maria said.

"Excellent. I will be flying back to my home tonight. In fact, I need to leave right now." The Wolf stood and put his arms out.

Maria, forcing another smile, stood and let The Wolf hug her.

"I need this resolved. Raul has many important family members in both cartels, Maria. I'd hate for them to get antsy. You do not want these people invading your pretty little beachside town and creating all kinds of chaos."

"You have my word I will get to the bottom of this, and quickly," Maria said. "I will leave first thing in the morning to head back and put out feelers."

"I trust you will do well." The Wolf gave her a quick hug before turning on his heels and snapping his fingers. "We leave. Now."

Maria walked The Wolf and his men to the door of the hotel, gave a quick wave before frowning and going up to her room.

She was exhausted. The few minutes she'd spent with The Wolf had tired her out.

Maria wasn't looking forward to going back to her hometown. She wanted to stay clear and let things settle first. She had a few locals there keeping watch for her. So far it looked like Cuba and the others hadn't found the treasure, which was good and bad.

If they found it she could take it from them and be in the wind, if possible.

Maria stripped down and decided to take a cold shower before making plans to leave in the morning.

She smiled, thinking if she should tell Ernie Patek and Baker Cioffi, who were also staying at this hotel, which she'd switched to. They were trying to stay hidden but she knew they were here. In fact, she had one of her men watching them at all times. If she wanted she could go down to the third floor and knock on their door.

Baker was a DEA agent, but he had no backup in Mexico. She was curious what his game was, but not curious enough to simply ask him.

Ernie was nothing in this game anymore. The fat man didn't know where the treasure was and had no use for Maria. He wasn't a threat so she'd kept him alive, even after what he'd done to her.

Ernie had given me the move to kill Raul, so I must thank him... before I kill him, too, Maria thought.

Maria decided to not tell the men when she left and see if they would be able to figure it out. There was no use in having them back in town and getting in her way.

Unless... Maria stepped into the shower and smiled.

Raul's death needed a scapegoat.

Ernie or Baker would suffice. It didn't matter which one it was, either. Perhaps they'd both done it. A conspiracy.

As she showered, Maria started to work out a plot that would make sense to The Wolf and keep the man from pointing a finger at her.

THREE

Baker opened the hotel door for the hundredth time. Ernie, who shared the adjoining room and insisted on keeping the doors open, pulled him back and slammed the door.

"What the hell are you doing? Bringing more attention to us?"

Baker sighed and sat down on the small couch. It smelled like musk and dirt. He couldn't give up the fact that the same person they tied up in the boat was staying at the same hotel. How the hell did that work out?

What were the chances?

Mexico City was a big place. Did everyone on the wrong side of the law choose this place? It seemed like a movie, where only bad guys checked in, and some never checked out.

Baker hadn't been in touch with his wife for a while and he knew she was worrying about him. But he didn't dare use the room phone in case someone was listening in and tracing the call.

He thought about going out and buying a burner, but Baker was too paranoid to even leave the room. The second he walked out, Baker was convinced he'd be shot. During his entire time in the agency, he never had been put in this situation. He was used to writing reports on cases that a child could have solved.

The cartel, Patek, being dragged to Mexico City. Baker wasn't prepared for that.

A hand fell on his shoulder and he was pulled back into the room. Ernie slammed the door and locked it and went back to watching some kind of soap opera-looking show on the television.

Baker rubbed his shoulder and sat on the other queen-sized bed and took in the situation. He tried looking at the bright side of things. At least there were two beds in the room. The last thing Baker wanted was to sleep next to Ernie. The guy snored like a bear with a chainsaw, and he was pretty sure the guy groped around when he slept.

The air conditioning was decent. If Baker had to pay for a room himself, it certainly wouldn't be in any place as near as nice as this hotel. He'd probably be soaked in sweat and swatting flies away.

Another good things was... there weren't any fucking good things about this situation. Who was he trying to kid? They were sitting at twice the elevation of Denver, sharing the same building with someone who was going to try to kill them, and if you walked outside the sun fried you in thirty seconds. Can't drink the water, although Ernie seemed to be immune to it.

"Do you even know what they're saying?" Baker asked, pointing to the television.

"I'll have you know my grasp of the Spanish language is pretty okay. Not to brag, but I also know a bit of Greek, French, Italian, and some Gaelic."

"None of that is in your file. If I recall, Mexico is the only other country you've been to. How'd you learn those other languages?"

Ernie paused the show. Apparently, the place had all the amenities including TiVo or whatever the hell it was called now.

"Rosetta Stone. Good for long plane rides. Gets boring after a while, though. I got an extra license if you want to try it."

Someone knocked on the door.

Baker stood and pressed his back against the wall, around the corner from the doorway, his gun pulled.

Ernie stared at him like he was an idiot.

"You hungry? I ordered room service. Maybe calm down a bit, huh?" Ernie headed toward the door.

"When did you order? I didn't hear you call."

"When you were staring into the hallway like a scared little mouse. Did it right on their app. You know, you seem to think we're in some third world country. Mexico City is beautiful and modern." Ernie lifted his cell and shook the screen at Baker. "Room service right from your damn phone."

Baker peeked around the corner, gun ready at his side as Ernie opened the door. Some teenager in a hotel uniform rolled in a food cart. The top of the cart was filled with plates and a bottle of tequila.

Baker holstered his weapon and stood out, smiling.

The kid rolled the cart in and waited, also smiling. Ernie thanked him, stuffed a few bills in the guy's shirt pocket and ushered him out the door.

"Now we're having a good time," Ernie said, walking into the bathroom. He came out with a couple body towels and hand towels. He held them up to Baker. "Best napkins around. And the greatest part is, you don't have to wash them."

Ernie draped the body towels across the bed and placed the mountain of food on them. He threw a hand towel at Baker and tucked his into his collar.

"Wait," Baker said, as Ernie was about to shove half a burrito into his mouth. "What if someone got to the food before it got to us?"

"What are you talking about?"

"Poison. What if Maria found out we were here and had the food poisoned. Shit, the cook could have even done it."

Ernie looked at Baker, took a massive bite of his burrito and chewed.

"Who would poison food? An animal, that's who. I don't care how bad you want someone dead, you don't fuck with food. Besides, she doesn't know we're here. I keep telling you that. There's no way. She had no idea we were coming here, just like we had no idea she would show up. We're good. We haven't even left the room. Not my choice, by the way."

Baker wanted to continue the argument, but the smell of all the different foods was making his stomach grumble.

"Fuck it," he said, more to himself than to Ernie.

He sat and grabbed a carne asada taco, waited a minute just to make sure Ernie didn't start foaming at the mouth, then ripped into the food like a starving dog.

Ernie took another bite of his burrito, after a swig of tequila, and paused. He coughed. Shaking it off, he continued chewing, then paused and coughed harder.

"You okay?" Baker asked.

As Ernie continued coughing, Baker dropped his taco and tried to spit out whatever was left in his mouth.

"Poison. Fucking poison. I told you, you stupid ass." Baker ran to the bathroom and stuck his finger down his throat, emptying his stomach.

When he came back out, Ernie was eating another burrito and laughing.

"You are way too gullible."

Baker was about to leap over his bed and tackle Ernie, when another knock came on the door.

Baker looked at Ernie, who had put his food down and was wiping his hands on the towel. What was once a white towel now looked like a couch from the 70s.

"Must have forgotten something. I thought the food was a little light."

Ernie opened the door. Baker, still pissed, sat at the edge of the bed and stared at the air conditioning unit, waiting for Ernie to come back with more food.

After a few seconds of silence, Baker turned.

Ernie stood by the television with a gun to his head. Next to him, Maria smiled as she pressed the gun harder against his head.

"Hello, both of you. I think we have a lot to talk about."

FOUR

Cuba was not happy. The first dive had come up empty, but he had several more planned in the next few days. They were at their second probable site, although he'd had high hopes for the first one.

How had Ernie Patek, of all people, fooled him?

Because you take him for granted. He looks like an idiot, he does idiotic things, but he is cunning. Ernie knows what he's doing and he fooled you, Cuba thought.

No one had spoken to him over the past few days. They'd all gone about their own business with the little space he'd given them. His men were watching them and he had cameras in most of the rooms so no one could escape.

Rick and JoJo were having some domestic issues and he tried to listen in whenever possible, because he felt more each day he was going to get JoJo on his side. The woman was amazing, and the more he chatted with her and the more he learned about her past, or what she wanted to tell about it, the more he was into her.

He knew it wasn't love. That was for suckers. No, it was a definite lust that was driving him toward her. As for Rick... if he needed to kill the man he supposed he would. Not only if Rick got in the way of the treasure but got in the way of his budding relationship with JoJo.

Alberto seemed to be brooding most of the time, waiting for the next treasure hunt so he could be on the water and in his element. The man was almost smiling now, standing at the controls of his boat, waiting for the divers to descend into the depths.

Cuba, JoJo, and one of his men were going to explore below, while everyone else waited.

Grace had her bikini on and was trying to get a suntan, even though there were thick clouds overhead. She also wasn't talking to him the past couple of days, buried in her own thoughts and world.

If I can find the treasure I'll let them all go, Cuba thought. *I won't need them anymore. I doubt they'll be able to find me once I disappear, either. I'll be in the wind.*

Except for maybe Rick, who might be trouble.

Cuba didn't want to waste anymore time. If this dive was unsuccessful, he'd need to immediately get to the next spot and try his luck there.

JoJo bent over to get her gear on and Cuba couldn't help but stare at her fine ass. When he glanced over to see Rick watching him with a frown, it made Cuba chuckle.

They dove down and couldn't find a wreck. Even using the hand-held metal detectors, there was nothing in this spot. Either the research Cuba had done was wrong, Ernie had screwed him over again or the storms over the years had moved what was left away from this spot.

Cuba didn't want to waste anymore time. He had them surface and strip out of their gear. "We need to refill the tanks and make sure everything is working properly for the next dive."

He pointed at Alberto. "Onward to the next coordinates, captain."

Alberto faintly grinned and gave Cuba a nod.

All Alberto needs is some positive affirmation he's the captain and he'll fall and stay in line, Cuba thought.

"How's it going?" Cuba asked Grace, sitting down next to her. He gave a quick nod to his men to let them know they needed to stay sharp, not only for outward threats but in case Rick or the captain decided this was the right time to try and overpower Cuba and his crew.

Grace frowned. "Fine."

Cuba leaned closer to her, not wanting to block what little sun was getting to her from above. "I need you on my side. Together we can get very rich. Understand?"

Grace was still frowning. "This isn't right and you know it."

"What isn't right?"

She sat up on her elbows. "We're your prisoners, which means when you do find the treasure, we're no longer needed. Expendable. You'll open the treasure chest, empty the contents and stuff our lifeless bodies inside and toss it back overboard."

Cuba shook his head. "No. You're my daughter. You know it. I guess you've always known it. I would never hurt you."

"Then let me go," Grace said. "Let them go, too."

Cuba was about to argue with her but stopped himself. Maybe she was right. He stared at JoJo and Rick, who seemed to be arguing again.

He needed them to find the treasure, but Grace was right. He was going to get rid of them once they had no more value to him.

Cuba stood and shouted for silence. When everyone was looking at him, he put up his hands.

"You are all no longer my prisoner, if that's what you think you were," he said. "As soon as we get back to the marina you are all free to go your own way. How does that sound?" Cuba looked down at Grace, who took off her sunglasses and stared at him.

"Not funny," Rick said.

Cuba shook his head. "Not a joke. I mean it. Grace has let me see what I've been doing was wrong. Forcing you to work for me without proper cooperation, without any benefit to you."

"Meaning what, exactly? We can walk away and you won't come after us? You know we're still going to try to find the treasure," JoJo said.

Grace cleared her throat. "What if we became a partnership? Collectively, it makes more sense to join together and find the treasure. Then we split it evenly. There should be more than enough for all of us to get rich."

Cuba smiled. What she said was true, and he did need them to help. "I agree. If we can come to an agreement like Grace said, we can all benefit. Before the cartel or Ernie Patek gets their hands on it. What do you say?" He held out his hand, making sure he was facing Rick first. He knew JoJo would be interested in staying.

Rick was staring at Cuba's hand. "How can we trust you?"

"I give you my word." Cuba motioned for his men to holster their weapons and relax.

Rick shook Cuba's hand but he didn't look happy.

When Cuba shook JoJo's hand, he made sure to let the touch linger. He could feel the electricity between them.

"Then it's settled. We work together." Grace stood. "Equal partners, which means I'm going down on the next dive, too."

Cuba was about to argue but decided not to. It wasn't worth the fight and creating a rift, when they'd all been very happy to agree to work together.

Until we find the treasure and I kill every last one of you, Cuba thought.

None of them could be trusted, not even Grace.

Alberto was smiling. "We're almost in position for divers."

Cuba gave a laugh, feeling good about his chances of being the last man standing in all of this.

FIVE

He wasn't stupid, just... naive.

For being her father, Grace would have thought Cuba would have more brain power than he did. She certainly didn't get her intelligence from her mother.

Grace wondered what she did get from Cuba. For a while now, she'd been thinking about how she reacted in social situations and how she seemed to enjoy putting herself into dangerous situations.

From as long as she could remember, Grace did what she wanted, not oblivious to the consequences, just not caring about them. No remorse. No guilt. She'd lived her life acting on impulse and without emotion.

She stole because she wanted it. She attacked because they deserved it. She took other people's cars on joy rides because it made her feel... not happy, but less under pressure. The danger of it all seemed to release a valve in her head and kept her from doing something even worse.

Why did she teach herself how to make a homemade taser? Not because she ever thought she'd have a use for it, but because she liked the idea of being able to defend herself in any situation.

It wasn't that she didn't feel emotions, she just experienced them differently from other people. And sometimes she didn't understand why people expected her to react a certain way.

Grace had gotten good at putting a mask on during daily life, pretending to be just another person like everyone else. Neuro-typical. Grace thought that was the word used to describe your everyday robot.

She watched as Cuba talked to everyone on the boat. Grace thought he was lying, but that may have been just because she would have lied in the same situation.

Hell, she was lying to her own father now.

Cuba had the muscle and the strength and he knew enough about the life he lived to be smart enough to keep himself on top. But when it came down to instincts, there was something missing. Him getting involved with Ernie Patek – Grace still thought of him as her father – was proof enough that he didn't have the best mind for the criminal underworld.

Grace laid back and put her earbuds in. She didn't play anything and kept the noise cancellation off. She'd found in the past that nothing gave people the confidence to speak freely when they saw someone with earbuds.

JoJo and Rick went off to the side and continued their personal arguments they'd been having daily. Cuba was going over coordinating with Alberto, who appeared to be getting calmer as time went on.

Initially, Alberto looked like he'd just gotten yanked out of bed, slapped in the face, and shook for an hour before going out into the world. She'd overheard talks about his prior dealings with the cartel, including the drug running up and down the coast. Grace figured Alberto would have more fortitude than he appeared to have.

Lucky for her, she'd guessed right.

Grace hadn't bought the whole afraid for his life attitude Alberto had exuded. She could almost see him put that mask on when Cuba first showed up and took them away. Grace had plenty of experiences with it, and plenty of masks for herself as well.

Two nights ago, once the current trip out to this dive was finalized, Grace approached Alberto. Rick and JoJo were outside, and Cuba was busy getting drunk in the other room with his men.

Alberto sat on one of her father's big, obnoxious chairs, sipping on a drink and staring out the window at the pool where JoJo and Rick were having it out again.

"Zoning out, or spying?" Grace asked as she sat next to him.

Alberto tapped lightly on the window.

"Bulletproof, I'm assuming. Can't hear anything through these." He turned to Grace. "Wouldn't mind hearing what was being said."

"The more you know kinda thing?"

"What do you want?"

"No need to get cranky with me. I'm on your side, remember?"

"You're the one who got us stuck in this place with Cuba, having to answer to him now."

"What if I said there was a way out?"

"I'd say tell me, then I'd most likely call bullshit. The guy has the manpower and the knowledge to get us to do what he wants. Despite his outward I'm-a-good-guy attitude, we both know the only person he cares about is himself. Maybe you. I haven't figured that dynamic out yet."

"Let me lay it out for you. We're under Cuba's thumb for now. The cartel seems to be having its own issues and are, at least for the moment, more concerned with that situation than with any of us. When that will change, who can say? But I know that even though Cuba has brass balls, he's not going to take on the cartel. It'll be a death sentence, even if he does make it out of the country. He'll try to go for the treasure fast. If this next dive doesn't pan out, we may be moving onto another site before we have a chance to breathe.

"JoJo and Rick are obviously focusing on their personal bullshit. So their focus isn't going to be one-hundred-percent on the treasure for now."

"Your point?"

"Cuba doesn't feel like he needs to watch his back for the time being. JoJo and Rick are in their own world. That leaves you and me as the only two people seeing the whole picture. That means we're playing with the advantage."

"Ok, Nancy Drew, what's your idea?"

Grace talked with Alberto while keeping an ear out for anybody – especially Cuba – coming in from the next room. Alberto listened, shook his head at parts until she cleared up his concerns, then sat back on the chair.

"Could work. Doesn't leave much room for error. And I'd be the one who'd get fucked if things went south. You've left yourself plenty of deniability in this scheme."

"I'm not going to lie. My number one concern is myself. But I'm coming to you with this because you're the only other person here I can trust with this. And you're the only one who would be able to help me pull it off. Even if JoJo and Rick were on spot and not constantly arguing, they wouldn't have the capacity to do it. You? I've heard stories about you. Are you in?"

Alberto remained silent for a while before slightly nodding his head and downing the rest of his drink.

Grace watched him now as he helped get things ready for the dive. The sun cooked her body and she hit play on her iPhone since nobody seemed to be talking about anything useful.

Alberto glanced her way and she winked at him.

Even though they were clear on the plan, Grace still was relying on him to put all the pieces in order. He was right that, if something went wrong, she could make herself look innocent and he'd take all the blame.

The question in her mind was, if he felt that way then what was he doing behind her back to try to flip the scales on her?

SIX

Ignacio was glad to be out of hospital, but now he knew things were going to get interesting. Likely not in a good way, either.

Catalina had been hanging around since she'd sold him out to the rest of the crew, acting like she cared about him. Especially when his mother was around. Ignacio knew better than to get his mother involved, because she'd only make it worse trying to protect him.

He didn't need her protection because he was already forming a plan in his head, one where he could escape with his family and the treasure.

The hard part was knowing who he could trust. There was no way he was able to pry open the lid to the treasure chest on his own. He'd tried several times.

Now he knew he'd never get near the treasure without someone following him.

Ignacio went home and let his mother coddle him for a few hours. He'd glance out the window and see one of the lower crew members watching the front door, and knew there'd be another on the rooftops in the back somewhere. They weren't going to let him get away, because they thought he had some secret information.

Which he did.

He'd need a partner, someone he could trust. Again... that didn't leave many options, if any.

Ignacio went into the kitchen when he smelled the soup his mother was cooking for dinner and smiled. It was his favorite.

"Can you run down to the corner store and buy a bag of tortilla chips? Are you feeling good enough, my son?"

Ignacio smiled. "Of course. A walk will do me good."

He was out the door and smiled when he saw it was now Arturo, who'd taken his place as the crew's leader, pacing with him across the street.

Instead of ignoring Arturo, he decided to have some fun.

Ignacio began to run down the street as fast as he could, even though he was hurting now and out of breath. He ducked into the corner store and walked calmly around, gathering the tortilla chips and a few other items.

Arturo ran right past the building and down the street, which made Ignacio chuckle.

He was halfway home with his food items when Arturo appeared, looking angry and jabbing his finger into Ignacio's chest.

"You think you're cute?" Arturo asked.

Ignacio shrugged and moved around Arturo, continuing down the street. "Catalina thinks so."

Even though the girl had sold Ignacio out and sided with his former crew, he still had a thing for her. It might just be puppy love. That was what he'd heard his Aunt Maria call it once when she thought he wasn't listening.

Catalina was beautiful but he knew she was devious. She'd been able to lure him into her web with smiles and seeming like she was interested in anything he said, which meant he'd told her most of his secrets.

He wondered if he would've told her about the treasure chest that night when he'd slipped out of hospital. Ignacio guessed he was lucky he hadn't blurted it out before she'd shown her true self, and Arturo and Leo had arrived to threaten him.

"What's in the bag?" Arturo asked, trying to grab it.

"My dinner. My mother sent me to the store. If you so much as break a chip I will end you. Understand?" Ignacio knew Arturo could probably beat him in a fair fight, but he wasn't intending to fight fairly. He had a roll of change wrapped in a sock in his back pocket, and he would use it to club the bigger kid if need be.

Arturo seemed to be thinking about his next move, taking a step back and making a fist.

"You can follow me all you want. Say mean things. Threaten me. Whatever, Arturo. But you do not mess with my family. My mother. If you try to ruin dinner all bets are off. You know what I can do," Ignacio said.

Not that he'd ever done much when it came to violence, but the threat had always been there. Ignacio was a big talker for such a small kid, and more than not the bigger kids respected him. Maybe a few even feared him because of the fake rumors he'd planted over the last couple of years. The supposed cruel things he'd done to rivals.

Arturo must've remembered some of them and knew he was now a rival, not so sure of himself.

"I'm not scared of you, but I respect your mother," Arturo said. He turned and walked away quickly.

"Yeah, I thought so." Ignacio went home and gave the bag to his mother, who thanked him.

"When is Aunt Maria coming over again? I need to ask her something."

His mother gave him an odd look. "Why? Ask me."

Ignacio shook his head. "It's nothing important. Just a memory I had about her, when I was little."

His mother smiled and tousled his thick head of hair. "You are still little, my little boy. Never grow up."

"I promise not to." Ignacio wanted to know about his aunt because he'd decided she would be the one he could confide in. Even though she worked with awful people, she was still family. She could still help Ignacio and his mother escape from Mexico with the treasure, and she'd even get a portion for herself for helping.

She was, after all, also family.

When it was obvious his mother either wasn't going to tell him or didn't know when his aunt would be visiting again, he went back to his room.

He sat on the window and saw Arturo and another of the crew back across the street.

If they're watching me and using manpower to do it, that means they aren't using their time for spying and gathering information, which means they're not earning any real money, Ignacio thought.

Now he remembered the American couple, Rick and JoJo, and wondered if they were still in town. Perhaps they were still looking for the treasure. He'd be able to pry more U.S. dollars from their pockets and lead them on a wild goose chase to find the treasure.

Ignacio decided to slip out tonight, very late, and find the Americans. He'd offer his services to them again but let them know none of his crew could be trusted.

Rick seemed unhinged enough he might try to fight Arturo or Leo if he was cornered, and Ignacio was going to make sure it happened.

He needed this crew off of his back and he needed to start making money again, even though he was sure the treasure chest was filled with untold riches that would make his life so much better and easier.

All he needed was Aunt Maria and Rick and JoJo to start making things happen for him.

SEVEN

DEA Agent Mike Benford wasn't happy. He'd been pulled from a big case in Dallas and down to the border of Mexico for this meeting within three hours.

When he saw fellow agent Nigel Tally already in the meeting room he frowned. He'd worked with Nigel once in the past on a few simple drug busts to move up the ladder for a grand trafficking case, but Nigel had been gone quickly.

Benford assumed he'd washed out or wasn't up to par with the team leads, who all seemed to be a bit racist to Benford. The leaders definitely hated Mexicans, but because Nigel was African they gave him a lot of bad jobs and made rude comments to the man.

"Hey, Mike. Any idea what's going on?" Nigel held out a hand and raised out of his chair. Benford shook hands and sat across from Nigel.

"None. I was up in Dallas. You?"

"San Diego. Small-time drug busts with a motorcycle gang." Nigel grinned. "Of course, since I'm the only black guy, I get to do the grunt work and stay hidden in the van and the one to get everyone coffee and lunch. Still better than when we worked together, however briefly."

Benford wanted to apologize for all of that but didn't have the words. He'd done nothing wrong, but still felt guilty he didn't stop them from harassing Nigel.

The door to the meeting room opened and two men walked in, both obviously supervisors by the way they walked and carried binders of files.

"Short and sweet, you two have been pulled off of your cases because we have an urgent problem," one of the men said, not even bothering to introduce himself or his colleague.

"You both, at one time or another, worked on the Ernie Patek case. Cases, in fact. You have also both worked with DEA Agent Baker Cioffi," the other man said.

Benford glanced at Nigel. Despite only working with the man for a short period of time, their paths must've crossed in the past. He couldn't remember when or where, though.

"And what do Cioffi and Patek have to do with us exactly?" Nigel asked.

"They're both somewhere in Mexico. We need you to find them, or at least find Cioffi," the first man said. He slid two files across the table. "It seems... he's AWOL."

Benford sat back. "Aren't there DEA agents in Mexico who could find him easier than us? I was making some progress."

Both of the supervisors looked at one another.

"They've been compromised," Nigel said and snapped his fingers. "The DEA office in Mexico has a rat. Maybe a couple. Am I right?"

"Perhaps. Right now we don't know much. Agent Cioffi was supposed to be on vacation but not in Mexico. He also missed the past week of work back home, and his wife has been trying to get in contact with him. It isn't looking good," the second man said.

"Maybe one of the cartels killed him," Benford said. Not to be rude but because it was highly likely. "Is there a reason he went down to Mexico in the first place?"

"We think because Ernie Patek was down there. We'd gotten a tip he'd gone down with his daughter and his crew but it was supposedly for a vacation," the first man said. "But with Patek, you know it is never just for pleasure."

"Do we think they're working together?" Nigel asked.

When both men looked at one another again, Benford had lost his patience. "Can we just get on with this? Tell us what we're doing and where we're going so I can get back to my normal undercover work and my normal life."

The first man tapped the file. "It's all here. All of the latest intel. You'll both be leaving on a flight within the hour. Don't check in with the DEA in Mexico City, either. This is strictly off the books. Rent a car in Mexico City and go to the small fishing village mentioned in the file. That was the last place we were able to track either Patek or Cioffi. No clue where they went from there but hopefully they're still in town."

The two supervisors left after dropping the plane tickets on the table. Different flights landing an hour apart.

"I'll land first," Benford said. "Meet you in the nearest lounge and we can go over what we studied on the way."

They each took a folder and left the meeting room.

"See you there," Nigel said and went the opposite way Benford was going.

This is going to be interesting, Benford thought.

Benford's flight was uneventful and he spent it reading through the material in the folder, wondering how much they were missing. He'd worked on the Ernie Patek cases on and off for years but they never really went anywhere. The big man was more slippery than an eel. Nothing seemed to stick to him. Not for long. He had the best lawyers and the best excuses and alibis.

Ernie Patek was definitely into a lot of illegal things but no one could pin anything definitive on the man.

The fact he was in Mexico meant something illegal was going down. So far no one had ever been able to prove it.

Benford wondered what was the deal with Baker Cioffi. He knew the man casually, having worked a couple of cases with him in the past. He wouldn't say they were friends. Maybe work buddies, a couple of guys thrown together to do lonely surveillance in strange cities that had spent some off duty time drinking a few beers and talking about their wives. Nothing more than that.

He supposed it was the same for Nigel Tally and Cioffi as well. Thrown together at one point to do some work.

Benford thought because he had done so much time working the Patek cases, and assumed also the same about Tally, it was the top reason they'd been given this job.

Was it to find a rogue agent or find something definitive on Patek? Maybe both? Benford had read the file several times but there didn't seem to be anything useful they could use today in it. Nothing that would lead them to the place where either Baker or Ernie were in Mexico.

If either was still even in Mexico.

He went to the lounge when his plane landed and went through the documents a third time, until Nigel arrived.

"I got nothing," Nigel said with a shrug of his shoulders. "I knew all of this. Maybe the part where Baker's wife is so sick was a shock, and it could be a motive for him going off the radar and off the playbook, but still... I worked with the guy for over a year. He seemed clean to me."

"Desperate times and all that," Benford said. "I already rented us a vehicle. Grab something to eat and drink for the road."

They each had one suitcase and one duffle bag, not knowing how long they'd be gone. Enough clothes and toothpaste to last a week and nothing more.

Benford was the lead on this, knowing more about Patek. Nigel seemed to know Cioffi better.

He wondered which man was going to be more important by the time they'd completed their task and hopped back on a plane heading north.

EIGHT

Maria broke the silence. Well, the silence besides Ernie's wheezing and Baker's foot tapping the floor.

"Funny we should wind up at the same place. I'd say great minds and all that, but you two are like that American couple. What are they called? Lauren and Hardon? I guess on the one hand I could thank you for not killing me on the boat. But on the other hand, that would be like thanking a child for not putting away its clothes."

"But we did leave you there. We spared your life. And Raul's. Technically you owe us," Ernie said, wincing as Maria pressed the gun harder against his head.

"You spared Raul's life for about half an hour."

"He's dead?" Baker asked.

"Killed him myself. I'd been planning on it for a while. If you really wanted to do me a favor, you would have killed him and kept me alive. Then I wouldn't be standing here right now with you two."

"Why are you here, anyway?" Ernie asked.

"Did you not just hear me? I killed my second-in-charge. And usually I'm allowed to do what I want as long as I don't try to punch above me. Raul had a lot of friends further up the chain of command. I didn't do anything against cartel rules, but I probably pissed a lot of people off who you don't want pissed at you. So, here I am. It looks like we're stuck together on a different kind of boat."

Maria frisked both of them, grabbed their guns and a belt buckle knife Ernie had, and motioned for them to sit on the beds.

She turned the armchair away from the television and sat facing them. She placed her weapon on the dresser and stared at both of them.

It was a risk, but Maria was betting she could get to the gun before they got to her if they decided to charge at her. Baker didn't appear to be in that great of shape. Looked like most of his DEA job was sitting behind a desk waiting for lunchtime. Ernie was a fat, wheezing mess of a human being, but she knew not to let the appearance fool her. Patek had plenty of experience dealing with the underground. She doubted if he'd ever read a book, but he knew the way of the streets, even if he'd been living in a mansion for the last couple decades.

Maria wanted them to feel as much at ease as possible. Having a gun trained on you tends to make things uncomfortable.

She'd been sitting at the bar in the lobby when she first saw them. The hotel was massive, with many floors. It was an open concept, so when you were in the lobby you could look straight up to the roof of the building, each floor with a wrought iron balcony and the room doors facing out toward the empty space.

Maria kept seeing a door open and close out of the corner of her eye, a couple floors up. Initially, she didn't think much about it and continued to sip her drink and watch the revolving doors at the entrance for anybody who she may have to avoid.

Again the same door opened, the light from the inside piercing the dimly lit, calming atmosphere around the bar. More importantly, seeming to shine directly into her eyes as if it had a vendetta against her.

Maria looked up at the hotel room, ready to curse the occupant. She caught just a glimpse of a face before the door closed.

No. It couldn't be. What were the chances of that? Maria thought.

When the waiter rolled the food tray to the same room and the door opened again, there was no denying who was there.

Ernie Patek and Baker, the DEA man. Together for some weird reason, and in Mexico City.

It seemed like the fates were pulling them together and Maria decided to find out why.

Ernie began to reach over to the food tray and Maria put her hand on the gun. He backed away, looking forlorn.

"Just wanted a piece of chicken."

"Get your chicken. But slowly, unless you want to chase it with a bullet."

"So what are we doing here?" Baker asked. "I mean, not literally here, although that's a good question. But what is the endgame?"

"I wasn't sure when I first decided to come up here. Killing the both of you wouldn't be the best idea. The gunshots would bounce all over every wall in this hotel. Don't take that to mean I won't. Try anything and I'll shoot you both and figure out the consequences later.

"But I've been thinking about it since we've reunited. I'll have to face my boss at some point. I can't hide forever, nor would I want to. What kind of life is that? I'd rather have them kill me. But I am hiding now, and I don't know if they're looking for me yet, or giving me a little grace time to be the one to get in contact."

"Can I have another–"

"Just eat your fucking food. Jesus Cristo." Maria waited for Ernie to fill his plate before continuing. "My point, before this grease trap decides it's time to take a shit, is that the cartel knows I'm hiding, trying to regroup. The last place they are going to look for me is the town I left. Which means the treasure is still in play. And with you, El Gordo, I can have it. Use some to buy myself back into the cartel's good graces, and the rest to take care of my sister and my ... and my sister."

"What about us? You need our help. What do we get out of it?" Baker asked.

"Technically, I don't need your help at all. Just Ernie's. But you might be useful if we run into law enforcement problems. At the least, you could make a good scapegoat. So what do you get out of it? Nothing. You get to live. And I'm not even sure about that. But if you help, you get to stay alive at least a little longer."

Ernie licked his fingers and shook his head.

"You still don't get it, do you?"

"What do I not get?"

"The map was bullshit. I'm sure there is treasure out in those waters, but I was never down here to try to find it. At least not as seriously as I made it seem. I was down here to put on a big show, get the rumors flying, and sell the map to the highest bidder. I should have been out of this country a long time ago."

"I know the map was faked. But you had the real location in your head. You said so."

"Smoke and mirrors," Ernie shrugged.

"Are you an idiot?" Baker screamed. "You just gave away the only fucking leverage we had."

"Not really. Like I said, there's no doubt there is treasure out there. I just have no clue where it is."

Maria stood up and pointed the gun at Ernie.

"Then your boyfriend is right. I don't need you." She racked the slide and pointed the gun at Ernie again.

"He's not my boyfriend, and you do need me. You just don't know it yet."

"Tell me."

"I don't show all my cards, sweet cheeks. But if I say Calle Hidalgo 85 that might give you an idea."

Maria stared at Ernie, then slowly lowered the gun and sat.

"You either just extended your life, or invited a very nasty death."

NINE

Another wasted day and all Rick had to show for it was a sunburn on top of his sunburn. He was glad he hadn't started doing drugs again, because the oppressive heat and humidity would have wilted him like a flower by now.

They'd been out on the boat for most of the day, and even with the sun dropping over the horizon, it was still too hot to be anywhere but in an air conditioned room.

JoJo looked exhausted. She'd been diving with Cuba and Grace, not taking a break even though they'd tried three wreck sites. Two of them actually had a shipwreck but the one they'd just surfaced from was nothing more than a large rock.

She still wasn't talking to Rick, other than a comment here or there. Mostly about food.

I need to regain her trust before it's too late, Rick thought.

He worried Cuba was going to swoop in and take her away, especially with the allure of treasure. While they were all supposedly now partners in this venture, Rick wasn't stupid enough to think Cuba was going to play fair.

JoJo was the wild card in all of this, because a couple of weeks ago Rick would've swore they were on the same page. They had the same focus and strive, and they were going to screw anyone and everyone who got between the two of them and the treasure.

Now... Rick wasn't so sure.

Cuba was looking up at the sky and smiling. Rick wanted to ask him why he had that dumb look on his face but decided not to. He didn't want to antagonize Cuba. No use in poking the bear.

"It will be a good night tonight. Not as warm. A nice ocean breeze, too," Cuba said. He swayed his hips and put his arms out, as if he was dancing with someone. He turned to JoJo and Grace. "Can you hear the music? Dance with me."

Rick wanted to groan. Was Cuba going to make such an obvious play at JoJo right in front of Rick?

Grace, laughing, stood and began dancing with her father.

Rick noticed JoJo was smiling as she watched them dance.

Alberto turned on music and sang along as he steered the boat back toward the marina.

Rick was about to stand and ask JoJo if she wanted to dance, hoping to break the awkward mood between them, but JoJo walked to Alberto and asked if he'd show her how to steer the boat.

Cuba was smiling as he stared at Rick.

Before this is all over with, I will knock him into tomorrow, Rick thought.

Rick knew he wasn't fooling anyone. Cuba was in much better shape, he was always on alert, and if Rick were being truly honest with himself... Cuba was the better match for JoJo.

He was trying not to feel sorry for himself but it wasn't working. He knew lingering drug withdrawal, the heat, having to sit on the boat while his girlfriend with a man trying to steal her away, it was all too much. Rick wanted to leave Mexico with JoJo and never look back.

Even without the treasure. He'd need to have a serious conversation with her as soon as he felt they'd gotten close to back to normal. Maybe she'd agree. There were other places and other people to rip off. The world was their oyster, right?

JoJo might be caught up in this, though. She enjoyed diving and the hunt for potential wealth. There was a solid case there was something out there, but none of them knew what it was or where it was.

Rick remembered Geraldo Rivera searching for Al Capone's secret vault and how that was such a bust on live TV. He felt like they could be involved in just such a thing here.

At least I have endless sunshine, Rick thought and frowned.

He knew he'd struggle to sleep tonight. His exposed skin was lobster red, and hot to the touch.

Cuba, Grace, JoJo and Alberto all had a nice tan. They weren't burnt at all.

Rick envied and hated them for that.

"What should we eat tonight?" Cuba asked Grace. "It's your turn to pick our meal."

"I want cheeseburgers and fries," Grace said and laughed. "I'm sick of expensive foods and small portions. Tonight I want a sloppy double cheeseburger with a gallon of ketchup on it. Maybe two."

Rick smiled. It seemed Grace was getting sick of her princess lifestyle, and maybe that had something to do with Cuba admitting he was her biological father. Maybe it had to do with her hanging out with Rick and JoJo, who were salt of the earth type people. Normal and caring.

Sure, they might also be greedy and grifters, but they had a good heart.

Rick wondered how all of this was going to play out. What would he do if JoJo didn't want to stop looking for the treasure? He knew he couldn't walk away by himself. His entire world revolved around her now, and he knew it.

JoJo likely knew it, too. She could use it against him if things got cruel between them.

Cuba pointed at Rick. "Cheeseburgers?"

Rick shrugged. "Sure."

"Then you are assigned the grill master tonight, Rick." Cuba smiled.

JoJo groaned. "No. Not a good idea unless you like charcoal hockey pucks. Rick burns everything on the grill."

"Not true. I like my meat cooked a bit, but not burnt," Rick said defensively.

JoJo smiled at Cuba. "I will grill the burgers. I'd like a couple of hot dogs, too."

Rick felt his face get hot when he saw the look JoJo was giving Cuba when she said hot dog and he didn't like it. There was something happening or something about to happen, and he'd be on the sidelines. He was going to be pushed out unless he stood up for himself.

Yeah, and make a fool of yourself. You are imagining things happening and nothing more. Loosen up and lighten up, bruh... you're acting insane, Rick thought.

He worried the withdrawals and the heavier need to score some drugs was messing with his mind. It was one thing to see every look between Cuba and JoJo as harmless, but lately they all seemed like a silent plot to kill him. Get rid of ol' Rick and split the treasure two ways.

I need to protect myself. Cover my own ass and not worry about anyone else, including JoJo, Rick thought.

All Rick could do was bide his time and hope he wasn't missing anything.

JoJo and Cuba were chatting while Grace stared off the way they'd come. Alberto had a smile on his face, piloting the boat back to the marina.

Rick wanted to act like all of this was normal, like they were explorers working together for a common goal. That all of this would be positive and good in the end.

He knew better, though. He felt like he was being scammed.

A scammer knows a scam when he sees one.

Rick knew as soon as Cuba felt Rick was no longer useful, he'd be killed and tossed overboard without a second thought.

TEN

Government pay is shit. Being on the right side of the law means crappy take-out, budgeting, and hoping your money lasts until the next paycheck. It wasn't bad pay, but it didn't lead to a very comfortable life.

George See, currently in a position that would be, at best, considered middle-management at the DEA, gripped the arm of the plane chair with one hand and squeezed the plastic cup of ice and two airplane bottles of vodka with the other.

Ten years giving Ernie Patek's people enough information to stay one step ahead of the law, he would have thought they could have gotten him at least a business class seat down to Mexico instead of being stuck with the rest of the cattle in coach.

George didn't even know why he needed to make the trip. Baker was an idiot who spent most of his time at a desk. He only went on a handful of field jobs. Yet somehow he'd gotten himself involved with not only Patek, but the fucking cartel. On his vacation.

The call had come in a couple days ago. The same distorted voice he'd always dealt with telling him the situation in Mexico.

George initially had asked why they couldn't just deal with his agent themselves. He had no specific ties to Baker, one way or another. If the guy never showed back up at headquarters, nobody would miss him.

But for whatever reason, his contact insisted that he fly down and take care of Baker himself. They didn't specify in what manner. George was pretty sure they were leaving it up to him whether to leave a body in Mexico, or bring Baker back alive and out of their way.

He would have told them to deal with it themselves, but a rogue agent on his watch would not look good for his next evaluation and possible promotion. That would cause the powers higher than him to maybe start looking into his background and George wasn't confident enough to think that they wouldn't find out about his many dealings with the same people the DEA had been trying to bring down.

Treason was not something he wanted pinned to his back.

The pilot came on the intercom.

"Sorry about that rough ride. It's something we call clear air turbulence. Unfortunately, not something we can predict. It should be smooth flying going forward, though. We'll be arriving in Mexico City in just under an hour."

No matter how many flights he'd been on, George could never understand how the pilots always sounded so calm. Even after this round of jostling, where some of the overhead compartments had opened and spilled out carry-on luggage onto people.

"Sir, can you put your seatbelt back on? Everything should be fine now, but just for safety's sake, we're asking people to keep buckled in," the flight attendant said.

"Fuck you," George said.

Being a DEA agent and carrying a gun on the plane meant he avoided the normal TSA security checkpoints. He had to go through another check out of sight of the public. It also meant that if there was no Air Marshal assigned to the flight, he would be, by default, the one to deal with any issues that came up.

The flight attendant gave him a look, but didn't respond. She knew who he was. He didn't need to flash a badge. In fact, that was the last thing he would have to do. The rest of the people on the plan weren't supposed to know who the marshal was.

George tipped back the rest of his drink and held out his empty cup to her. She took it with a grimace and walked away.

He shouldn't have been drinking on the plane, either, but fuck that. He'd never been on a plane sober and wasn't going to break that streak now.

White knuckle flier. Look that up in the dictionary and find his picture.

George brought up the web browser on his phone and waited for the slow plane WiFi to load his messages.

I should have taken a train, George thought. *Trains don't plummet to the ground at hundreds of miles an hour.*

The usual bullshit work messages popped up, which he ignored. He opened up his second messaging app, the one that was encrypted from end to end, and saw one message pending.

Subject on the move. Driver will be waiting. Mexico City no longer contact point.

George put his phone down.

Nothing ever was easy. Especially when it came to playing both sides of the law. One paid better, but it came with unpredictability and always the chance of death.

He wasn't afraid of dying. In some ways, he welcomed it. George had no family, never was married, no kids, and nothing that would make him miss living. But he did hate being inconvenienced. And for some reason, he hated the thought of going out in a plane crash. It seemed stupid and undignified.

Maybe when he intercepted Baker, he'd make sure he wouldn't be coming back.

George picked up the phone, sent a message back, and put it back down.

The anonymous voice on the phone hadn't told him much other than Baker was sticking his nose into places it didn't belong. They needed him gone or really gone, but didn't want the blood of a DEA agent on their hands.

It was a strange conversation, now that George thought back on it as the plane banked and started its descent.

Usually the voice on the other end of the line was more fluid, conversational. Granted, it sounded like a robot because of the distortion, but there was a flow to their exchange of information.

This one was more choppy, like someone trying to think of the right words every other sentence.

George figured he was dealing with someone else from Patek's crew. Though after ten years of the same person, he had to wonder what happened. Usually when someone stops calling in this line of work, it didn't mean anything good.

The plane landed without issue, and George grabbed his carry-on before the plane came to a stop and pushed his way to the front of the plane.

The flight attendant he'd told to fuck off gave him a look he didn't appreciate before telling the passengers to remain seated until the plane came to a full stop. George glared at her, daring her to tell him to go back to his seat.

She didn't.

George navigated his way through the terminal and outside, where a black SUV waited with a driver holding a card with his name on it.

The driver opened the back door and George slid in. The door shut and locked, which confused him until he saw the man across from him.

"Who the fuck are you?"

"Welcome to Mexico, Mr. See. My name is Diego Santiago. And I believe your agent had a part in killing my brother, Raul."

ELEVEN

The last dive had been too much for JoJo. She'd never let on that it had worn her out, but she knew she'd need a long, hot shower and a few pills for the pain. The worry was that she'd stiffen up overnight and be unable to walk normally tomorrow.

JoJo never wanted to look weak, but her age was starting to catch up with her now.

She knew Cuba was feeling it, too. It was never a good idea to have so many dives in such a short amount of time, but they were under the gun when it came to finding the treasure.

Patek and Maria had disappeared. For now. JoJo knew they might be lurking nearby, waiting for this crew to do all of the hard work. The heavy lifting, as Rick liked to say.

Rick would need to be dealt with soon, too. JoJo had a strong bond with him. They'd been through a lot together. Had each other's back. Pulled off some nice scams since they hooked up, too. But...

She wasn't in love with Rick. Never had been. They'd been physical but it was mostly after a successful grift, wrapped up in the high of the moment. Feeling like they were invincible. Like they were still kids finding their way, and nothing could stop them.

Except the drugs were going to stop Rick. She knew it. She felt it.

He might not be using again, not at the moment, but it was going to be soon. She saw it in his hopeless eyes, especially since Cuba had entered their group dynamic.

Rick had been pushed to the side, a cuckold in their life.

JoJo knew she was attracted to Cuba, and she knew flirting with the man was only going to keep her alive that much longer, but she wasn't interested in Cuba for anything other than a working relationship.

Once all of this is done, the goal is to get my share of the treasure and more, and get as far away from Cuba and Grace as humanly possible, JoJo thought.

She wondered if Rick would be taking that trip with her, too.

She'd never do anything to hurt Rick. Her worry was that he'd hurt himself, and overdose. Being so deep into drugs again he'd make a fatal mistake that might cost either of them their lives, and she wasn't going to stand for that.

JoJo needed to make a decision.

She knew confronting Rick would do no good. She'd done it plenty of times in the past, and he always denied it or made an excuse. She'd been happy when he'd kicked the habit, but knew the truth: an addict was always going to be an addict.

There was no magic cure for Rick, only the constant fight and struggle to keep clean another minute, another hour, another day.

JoJo had stripped down to her panties when she heard the knock on the door.

Knowing it couldn't be Rick, since he'd just enter, she slipped on a robe and asked who it was.

"Cuba."

"I'm busy. Come back later," JoJo said.

"I'd like to speak to you now," Cuba said. "Rick and Grace are busy at the pool. It will give us a few minutes to have a conversation we need to have."

JoJo hesitated. She wasn't sure which conversation Cuba was talking about exactly, but none of them were going to be good. This would all just muddy the waters even further.

She opened the door and Cuba entered, glancing at her in the robe.

"I was about to take a shower," JoJo said.

Cuba smiled. "I need one, too. Not only to get the salt water off of my skin but to soothe my aching muscles. I'm not as young as I once was. Maybe tomorrow you can remind me of that, especially if we do more than two dives."

"How many more spots do we have left to check?" JoJo asked. She figured Cuba was now just picking random spots to search, based on shipwrecks that were well-known, or places he was guessing on.

Half the dives had produced nothing, not even rotting timber.

JoJo wanted to go to the window and look down at the pool area. She was suddenly jealous Rick was out there with Grace, who was likely wearing a thong bikini and too-tight top.

I could be with Cuba and Rick could be with Grace and we'd all be happy, JoJo thought, knowing it was a lie. In no real world situation could any of that happen. Grace would use Rick up and throw him away, and only give the effort if she thought Rick had something valuable, which he didn't possess.

"What do you want to talk about?" JoJo asked, still standing. She was about to sit on the edge of the bed but thought it might be too inviting for Cuba to join her. She didn't trust him but she also didn't trust herself.

Cuba stepped closer to her. Too close. She could smell his deodorant mixed with his natural animal smell. JoJo thought she could get lost in that, especially in a passionate romp in bed.

JoJo, disgusted with herself, turned and walked to the window.

"I'm out of options, if we're being honest. I have nowhere else to dive," Cuba said. He sat on the bed and JoJo heard the sound of the mattress squeak.

Rick and JoJo had joked about how noisy it would be if they had sex on the bed, mostly Rick saying it, but so far they hadn't done it. They were both too prideful and hurt by the other to have makeup sex.

"Then we need to find Ernie Patek. He has to know where the treasure is," JoJo said. "Even... what the treasure actually is. Right?"

"It's our only real option, but I don't know how far he went." Cuba sighed. "He's still in Mexico. I know that for certain. I have friends who have been monitoring the crossings and the airlines."

"As soon as he uses a credit card, we'll find him," JoJo said.

Cuba shook his head. "He has many fake credit cards. So many accounts that even I don't know all of them, and he knows I'm not on his side anymore, so he'll use a secret one from the many secret ones he has."

JoJo was about to speak but she looked down at the pool and saw Grace and Rick laughing, both sitting inches from one another on the step in the pool.

Her tits are in his face. That little bitch, JoJo thought.

Rick seemed to be enjoying the view, too.

Cuba was up and moving. JoJo turned in time to see him moving in for a kiss.

She put up her hand and blocked Cuba.

"I don't think so. We need to remain professional. Nothing else. We're here for the treasure, remember?" JoJo turned back to the window and looked down at Grace and Rick, smiling and laughing together.

"We could be very good for one another," Cuba said quietly.

JoJo shrugged her shoulders. "I'm sure we could have a lot of fun together. But right now… it's not meant to be. Maybe once this is all over we can revisit this. Until then… please leave. In the morning we need to focus on finding Patek."

She didn't feel Cuba move right away, but after a few heartbeats she heard him shuffle across the floor and open her door.

"JoJo… I've never met–"

"Good night, Cuba."

TWELVE

Grace saw the light go out in JoJo's room. She'd noticed the curtains parting multiple times as Grace sat with Rick at the pool. That woman was one confused and torn person.

Grace had seen the way JoJo looked at Cuba, and definitely had noticed Cuba's hardcore flirting, which was gross. But Grace assumed, because of the long relationship JoJo and Rick had, that those ties were harder to break.

JoJo would eventually give in to Cuba's advances. Grace had no doubt about that. And it may be sooner than later. The way Rick pretended to laugh and have a good time at the pool with her was so transparent.

His eyes looked haunted and distant. His smile and laugh was almost like a pre-programmed defense mechanism.

Sucked for Rick, but it helped Grace when it came to her plan.

So far, only Alberto knew the details, and they had discussed it a few times since she'd initially brought it up. Both agreed they needed a third person to pull it off.

Rick was the only option.

There wouldn't have been another person if everything was chill between him and JoJo. So Rick's misfortune was Grace's gain. She couldn't risk bringing JoJo into it when her father was trying to make his moves on her and watching her every moment. Especially her ass.

Gross.

"What do you think of my father?" Grace asked.

Rick's breath hitched and his feet stopped kicking in the water for a moment longer.

"Is this a trick question? Did he send you out here to be all nice and then try to pump me for info?"

"Oh yeah, because me and him really get along so well. I'd be more worried about him getting close with your girl than the two of us forming a father/daughter bond. What I'm asking is if you trust him to follow through with his promises."

Rick looked out into the darkness. Grace thought she caught a glimpse of his eyes watering.

Great, I don't need this guy to go all bitch on me right now, Grace thought.

"No. And even if he did, I don't trust him to not break up my relationship."

"It takes two when it comes to that."

"It takes mostly one when that person is suddenly a very rich, attractive man."

"So what are you going to do about it?" Grace asked.

"What can I do about it? I don't know if you've noticed, but I'm not John Wick. He has the advantages from any position you look at."

"So you're just going to sit back and let whatever happens happen? I haven't known JoJo very long, but she doesn't seem the type of person who would get together with someone with no drive."

"A pussy, you mean?"

Grace looked at Rick and shrugged, not wanting to set him off, or more likely make him cry, by agreeing with him.

"I don't know what happened to me. I used to be a pretty good Fe ... person. Well, not counting the side deals I was involved with. But I used to be able to act instantly, to know the best way to go in a situation, to have control over almost everything."

"Drugs."

"What?"

"You go into drugs and it fucked up your life. It's not exactly a new story."

"How do you know anything about that?"

"Look, Rick. I'm smart. Like, super smart. You wouldn't know it looking at me or how I act most of the time, but believe me when I say I'm the smartest person here. That's something I can hide when I want or need to. Addicts can't hide their problems. Even when they're clean. And especially when an addict helps save a small Mexican boy with a gunshot wound by giving him heroin."

"Oh yeah, that. I forgot you were there for a second."

"I'm good at being forgotten when I need to be."

"I guess that's kind of what's caused this issue with JoJo. Even though I didn't relapse, she's acting like I did. It's bullshit."

"She's acting like you did because you might as well have. People like you won't understand that you do just as much, if not more, damage to the people around you as you do to yourself."

Rick kicked at the water a little too hard and an arc flew up and landed on them.

"Is this what you came out here for? To give me a lecture? Throw your father's flirting and my girlfriend's obvious interest in my face? If that's it, you can find another place to sit. I don't need everybody coming down on me. I'm stressed enough as it is. These dives. The heat. The constant wondering about when I might feel a gun pressed to the back of my head. I don't need any of this. I didn't ask for it. I just want things to go back to how it was before this treasure bullshit fell into our laps."

Grace leaned forward, making sure to squeeze her arms against the sides of her chest. A little flirting never hurt when it came to convincing someone to do something.

"What if I told you I had an idea to get all of us out of this? Nothing that would keep us looking over our shoulders afterwards. A clean slate. You could work on getting yourself and your relationship back in order. And we would all come away richer than we are now. Not necessarily change your life money, but enough to be comfortable for a while."

Grace was concerned she'd lost Rick in the middle of her cleavage and would have to repeat herself, but he shook off his stare after a moment and looked her in the eyes.

"I'd say that I'm listening."

Grace glanced over at JoJo's room, making sure the curtains weren't parted. She had nothing against her, but she was too close to Cuba to be brought into the plan. Her father would have to have no idea what was going on in order for Grace's plan to work.

Before she'd found out he was her father, she'd still been around him as Ernie's daughter. The man had a nose like a bloodhound. He could sniff out a betrayal miles away. Anyone, even if they weren't fully on his side, wouldn't have to say anything to him. If they were involved in something he wasn't aware of, he would know. Only Grace, as far she was aware, was able to cloak her intentions from him.

Maybe it ran in the family.

Grace took another quick look around, making sure none of Cuba's men, or Cuba himself, were lurking.

She leaned back toward Rick, not trying to be sexy this time, and told him what she'd said to Alberto.

She let him in that Alberto was already on board, but left out a couple key details.

As much as she thought she could trust Rick, he was straddling the line between sobriety and full-blown addiction. If anything went wrong with him, he wouldn't know the most important parts.

Only Grace knew everything, and she was fine with that.

THIRTEEN

Leo was standing in front of the bodega across the street. Ignacio figured it was Leo's turn to babysit and make sure Ignacio didn't leave his home.

They were scared of him. Still. Even though they'd taken his power and his crew, they still worried he'd get it all back.

Ignacio was going to take it all back, too. He just needed to set a few things in motion. Without Arturo, Leo and Catalina in his way he could reorganize the rest of his crew.

He had a few things to work out first, though.

Should he let his Aunt Maria in on any of this? He knew she wasn't who she pretended to be. He'd heard more than rumors on the street over the years. She was not only a player in the cartel, but she was a leader. Aunt Maria had gotten this far because she was ruthless. She did what needed to be done, too.

Ignacio worried his mother would be upset if her son brought in not only his aunt but the cartel. He was smart enough to know whatever was in the treasure chest would go to them and he'd get a small taste of it.

No. It was too risky to involve anyone else in this plan. Maybe if he ran into Rick and his super hot MILF, JoJo. They'd be able to help.

But again... at a big cost.

He stared down at Leo on the corner, who was glancing up at the window every now and then. Ignacio kept his bedroom light off but Leo had to know he was up here and watching. Waiting.

What would Aunt Maria do? What would the cartel do in this situation, being watched by the enemy? I need to be active and not reactive, Ignacio thought. He remembered that idea from Rick, who'd said it in his presence weeks ago.

He wondered where Rick and JoJo were right now. Wondered if they'd not only forgotten about him, but were still using his crew to try and find the treasure. It would be ironic if they'd done that, since he knew where the treasure chest was.

Ignacio had a lot to think about and he wished he could take a long walk on the beach and figure it all out.

Why can't I? Let Leo follow me. I'm not going anywhere I can't be, he thought.

He told his mother he was going for a walk and was out the door before she had time to protest. He'd taken his light jacket, knowing she'd call after him if he did not.

Ignacio didn't try to sneak down the street. He still had his pride. He walked boldly, saying hello to people and acting like he had no worries.

Leo began following from across the street.

Ignacio stopped at a *changarro* and ordered a *molote*, which he ate while standing near the cart and dipping it into a small cup of salsa.

He smiled because Leo wasn't sure what to do, still on the other side of the street, trying to blend into the shadows, as if Ignacio hadn't already seen him.

Ignacio took a step toward Leo and smiled. "Hey, are you hungry, Leo?"

Leo took a couple of steps as if he was going to run away, but then he stepped out into the road and shrugged.

Ignacio knew they'd been friends for a long time, growing up together on these streets, and Leo's family was dirt poor. At least Ignacio had his Aunt Maria to sometimes bring food with her and give his mother some money for groceries and the rent.

He bought another *molote* and handed it to Leo as he walked over.

"Thank you," Leo said quietly, not making eye contact. "I haven't eaten in a couple of days."

Ignacio used to take care of Leo and most of the other boys and girls. He remembered the time he'd broken into a restaurant on the other side of town, a couple of hours after they'd finished making tortillas for the next day and locked up.

He'd taken as much as he could carry and his crew had feasted the next morning, day and night. Everyone had been well-fed for once in a long time and they'd taken whatever was left home to their own families.

Ignacio had been proud of that moment.

"I hope Arturo is taking care of my crew," Ignacio said.

Leo kept silent as he finished the food quickly.

Ignacio let Leo take a sip of his juice to wash it down. "Why are you following me? Is Arturo worried about me?"

"I don't really know. We're all taking turns to make sure you don't come at him, I guess," Leo said.

Ignacio smiled because Arturo was scared. "Why does he think I'd come after him?"

"No, not directly. He thinks you'll try to recruit some of his crew and work against us."

"His crew? I'm the one who did all of the work putting it together," Ignacio said. "And I will form another, better crew. Come with me."

Leo shook his head. "I can't. I'm loyal to Arturo."

"After all I've done for you?" Ignacio asked, annoyed.

"I'm sorry. Arturo is the new boss. I do what he says, and I'll have to tell him what you said to me."

Ignacio threw up his hands in disgust and started to walk away.

"Hey, wait... where are you going?" Leo asked.

"Isn't that your job to figure out, working for Arturo? Since he's so scared of me and what I'm capable of," Ignacio said, picking up his pace and heading toward the beach.

"He's not scared of you. He's worried you'll screw up his big plans, which is to not only take over this town but this area and the next town and the next." Leo was now walking next to Ignacio. "He doesn't want you messing it up for him. He thinks you'll never fall in line and work under his command."

Leo grabbed Ignacio by the arm and stopped him. "He wants to kill you."

Ignacio chuckled. "Arturo thinks he can kill me?"

"No. He thinks I can. Maybe Catalina. He's going to ask us to do it. Soon, I fear."

"Why are you telling me this?"

"So that you can leave. Go to live with your aunt or another family member. You have options. Arturo wanted to kill you and your mother, but we said that would never happen. You don't mess with a person's family. Right?" Leo shook his head again.

"I need you to give Arturo a message from me," Ignacio said, the anger rising inside. "He'll understand this one loud and clear, too."

"Ok."

Ignacio looked around. They weren't at the beach yet but only a block away. The streetlights on this road had been broken months ago with rocks but the town had yet to replace them. You knew better than to be hanging around in this area, anyway.

"Catalina will be next," Ignacio said, slipping the knife he always carried in his light jacket out and plunging it to the hilt into Leo's stomach.

Leo tried to pull away but Ignacio grabbed him by the back of the head and made sure the knife was still inside him, and now he twisted it a few times.

"You betrayed me, Leo. Catalina did, too. She will die next, before I kill Arturo and string him up," Ignacio said. "And you know the sad part about all of this?"

Leo had no answer, his eyes fluttering and the moan escaping from his throat sounding like a cat who'd been run over.

"The treasure. I have it. I know exactly where it is, and I won't be sharing it with anyone not loyal to me," Leo said. He pulled the knife out and stabbed Leo, his friend who he'd taken care of for so many years, a dozen times until the knife blade broke.

Ignacio had never killed anyone before, never intended to do it, but the rage had been unleashed.

Now he needed to clean up and plan for Catalina's demise next.

FOURTEEN

Agent Nigel Tally walked into baggage claim with his arms full of airport food. He'd almost dropped the sodas a few times while weaving his way through the crazy throng of people. He wasn't too worried about the Diet Coke, but if he dropped his Mountain Dew Baja Blast he would have been really upset.

Mike was waiting for him, sitting on one of the uncomfortable plastic chairs by the exit. Nigel always thought the airports purposely made the baggage claim seats significantly more uncomfortable than the seats at the terminals. Leaving an airport just wasn't profitable for them. Better to get the people out as quickly as possible.

He went over to Mike and leaned down, gesturing for him to relieve him of the containers of food. Once he was freed up and sure his drink wasn't going to be a casualty on the floor, Nigel sat next to Mike and drank half of it before taking a look around.

Nigel looked down at the suitcase in front of Mike, at the endlessly circling baggage carousel, and back at the suitcase.

"Where's my bag?" Nigel asked.

Mike shrugged and took a sip of his gross diet drink.

"Over there somewhere. It'll come around again."

"You didn't grab my suitcase?"

"Not supposed to touch someone else's bag. It's against TSA rules or something."

Nigel was pretty sure that wasn't it, and that Mike just was too lazy to wait around for his suitcase to show up. But he wasn't sure. In a way, it made sense. Random searches started with questions like 'have you had your suitcase in your possession the entire time.' He'd have to look up the rules before laying into Mike for making him do all the work and have to go stand like a moron at the rotating belt and wait for his bag.

"When did you start at the Agency?" Nigel asked.

Mike finished his Coke and placed the container under his seat, which was two feet away from the trash bin.

"Almost ten years now. Seems like a lifetime."

Nigel nodded and turned away before Mike saw the look of disgust on his face. Nigel was going on his fifteenth year, and if everything went according to plan, he would be able to retire soon.

He had seniority on this slob, yet he was going around like his errand boy. This would have to be brought up and cut down soon before it turned into a dynamic between them that Nigel wasn't willing to accept.

Mike opened his container and frowned.

"What the fuck? Did you tell them extra ketchup on the burger? This is just a normal amount. Shit, it might be less than a normal amount. What the hell?"

It took Nigel a moment to make sure he wasn't going to puke as Mike ran a finger through the pool of ketchup on the bottom and popped it into his mouth.

They had worked together a few times in the past, but never out in the field for more than half a day. Usually they were put together to read through reports and evidence and come up with solutions that other agents weren't able to. Nigel had always liked Mike but, like a couple that had been dating for a while and moved in with each other, he was seeing a side of the guy he found disgusting.

Nigel saw his suitcase come out from the insides of the baggage claim, the multiple tags from all the places he'd been a giveaway. He walked over, grabbed it, and sat down.

Checking the lock he'd put on it for signs of tampering, he sat back convinced nobody had attempted to open it at any point between getting checked and arriving here in Mexico City.

"Why'd we have to fly into this city? This elevation is killing me. And it's like an eight-hundred hour drive to where we're supposed to be. I'm going to melt when we walk outside."

"Have you always been this annoying, or does travel not agree with you?" Nigel asked.

"What are you talking about?" Mike said through a mouthful of fries.

"Nothing. You ready to go?"

Mike sopped up the rest of his disgusting ketchup with the remaining fries and showed them in his already full mouth. He placed the empty container under his seat next to the Diet Coke.

"I guess so. The car out there?"

Nigel looked outside at the couple dozen town cars that looked exactly the same. Nobody was holding up a sign with their names, nor did Nigel expect that. When you were flying into another country on active duty with an intelligence agency the last thing you did was announce it.

"We'll know when we go outside. Stop being a pussy about the heat and the elevation and let's get going. Clean up your mess, also. Your parents aren't employed here."

Mike gave him a blank stare. Nigel shook his head and stood, lifting the handle of his suitcase and spinning it behind him. He'd leave this slob behind if he had to. He was fully qualified to deal with this Baker issue by himself. If anything, Mike would find a way to screw it up.

Nigel was about to chastise Mike when he looked to the right outside of the windows.

"What the fuck?"

Mike was standing and grabbing his luggage, wiping his hands on his pants.

"What?"

"Is that ... Come here." Nigel grabbed Mike by his collar and pulled him to his side. He pointed where he was looking. "Is that Agent See?"

They both watched as the man outside got into a black SUV, which then pulled away from the curb, cutting off traffic and causing a litany of horns beeping.

"Is it? I didn't catch his face."

"I'm almost certain that was him. What is doing here? Did the Agency send him down also? Like a backup or something?"

"I guess it's possible. They certainly wouldn't have told us if that was the case. Compartmentalization and all that."

"It makes no sense. We're down here to find a desk jockey gone rogue. Why the need for backup?"

"Um. I think we're going to have more questions than that," Mike said.

"What do you mean?"

"Nine o'clock."

Nigel turned to his left and watched three people crossing from the parking lot to the waiting area, heading toward another waiting SUV.

"Holy shit," Nigel said.

Maria Guerrero, Ernie Patek, and Baker Cioffi, almost walking hand in hand, disappeared into the SUV, which sped off almost as fast as the one Agent See got into.

Nigel and Mike looked at each other.

"I'd say we should follow one of them, but I have a feeling we're all going to the same place," Nigel said.

Mike followed him outside to the car where the driver waited for them, making a motion to show he was the one the Agency had sent to pick them up.

Nigel didn't know what the hell was going on, or why everybody involved – or presumably involved – in this Baker fiasco had shown up at the same place and same time.

At least they were tailing and not being tailed. Nigel knew from experience that it wasn't always good to be first in line.

FIFTEEN

Ernie wasn't too happy. He knew with Maria involved he was no longer going to be the boss, he was no longer calling the shots. Baker was easy enough to control. He'd do whatever Maria said, as long as it was spun to be a good thing for Baker.

Maria was never going to fall into that trap. She was going to spot Ernie coming from the wrong direction from a mile away. She'd already let it be known he wasn't fooling her.

"We need to figure out what Cuba is doing," Ernie said to Maria. "How many men do you have at your disposal that can find him?"

Maria glanced at Ernie sideways and sighed. "Never mind how many men I have. How many do you have? It seems like Cuba and all of your men have abandoned you."

"It does seem that way," Ernie said. He was staring out the window of the SUV. Maria was sitting between him and Baker, which seemed odd. She held all of the cards, so he guessed she could sit wherever she wanted.

Baker had been quiet on the plane ride and now in the car on the way back to town. He seemed preoccupied but Ernie wasn't going to pick his brain in front of Maria. Maybe if they got a second alone.

"I'm hungry. Anyone else?" Ernie asked.

Maria sighed again. "You're always hungry."

"Is that a fat joke?"

Maria shook her head. "Merely an observation. When we arrive at my villa we'll have the cooks prepare us some food."

Ernie liked the sound of that. He'd eaten in the airport in Mexico City before they boarded the plane, and had eaten a couple of bags of peanuts on the flight. Not nearly enough food for him.

He was also very nervous about how this was all going to play out. He had no delusion that Maria was going to let them go if the treasure was found.

"I need to call my wife," Baker said. It was the first words he'd spoken in hours.

"No." Maria glanced at Ernie again. "No one makes any phone calls. Got it?"

"I was actually thinking about doing something radical," Ernie said.

"What, skip a meal?" Maria laughed at her joke.

"What if I called Cuba?" Ernie asked.

Now Maria was staring at him. "Why in Hell would you do that?"

Ernie smiled. "He wouldn't be expecting it. Maybe he gives us a clue, since he might be the only one right now who knows where the treasure is. Hell, he might have even found it. I've known him for a long time. He has many tells, and I think even on a phone call I can feel him out."

"Worth a try," Baker said. "And I need to call my wife. I wasn't asking for your permission."

Maria at first didn't say a word. She'd taken their phones from them before they boarded the plane. Rummaging through her bag, she frowned. "If either of you are playing me, I will personally chop off your balls and stuff them in the other one's mouth."

"I don't want his balls in my mouth," Ernie said and leaned forward, waving at Baker. "No offense."

"None taken," Baker said.

Maria held up their phones. "One at a time."

"I go first," Baker said, snatching his phone and dialing.

Ernie wasn't in a hurry to call Cuba. He really wasn't sure what he'd even say, other than hello. Ask him how it was going. If he knew where Grace was. How much treasure he'd stolen from Ernie.

Baker was talking quietly to his wife, but Ernie could hear every word. He didn't think they were necessarily fighting, but she was pressing him.

"I'll explain everything when I get home. I know, I know. I missed your appointments. Tell your brother I'm sorry and I owe him a dinner or two. When I get back I can let you know, but right now I'm pressed for time. I gotta go. The boss is coming down the hall and he needs my report," Baker said. "No. You know I can't tell you anything. I'm in a foreign country. It's very dangerous but this might be my last trip for work, so there's that. We'll have plenty of time afterward. I might even take a long extended vacation. Stop worrying. You're going to be fine."

Ernie leaned closer to Maria. "His wife is very sick. Cancer or something awful like that. He came down here to find the treasure and go home a rich man, able to afford all of her medical bills."

Maria said nothing, staring at Ernie.

She was very pretty and he had the insane idea to lean over and try to kiss her, but he knew she'd likely break his nose.

Baker disconnected the call and handed Maria his phone back.

Now it was Ernie's turn.

He dialed Cuba and it rang four times. He was about to disconnect and not bother to leave a voicemail but Cuba answered with one of his annoyed *Yeah? What*? As if he didn't know who was calling.

"Hey, buddy. How's it going?" Ernie asked with a smile, giving Maria a thumb's up.

There was a pause on the other end. Maybe Cuba really didn't know who it was at first. "Hey, Ernie."

Ernie knew it meant there were other people in the room with Cuba, people involved in all of this. Grace? Others?

"Just checking in and seeing what's going on. Still in Mexico? Diving much?" Ernie asked.

"I do enjoy a good dive. How about you? Eating a lot?"

Ernie chuckled. "I do enjoy a good meal. We should do lunch and catch up. It's been far too long, right?"

"I'd say it has been. Are you still in town or did you run off somewhere?" Cuba asked.

Ernie smiled. It meant Cuba hadn't left town. It also meant he was still looking. He hadn't found the treasure yet. "I'm still around. Name the place and we can meet. Have some empanadas or tacos. I think a couple of towns over they even have a McDonalds. Whatever you're in the mood for, buddy."

"Who are you with?" Cuba asked.

"No one. Just me. Who are you with?"

"No one, either," Cuba said. It was obvious they were both lying to the other one. "What happened to the DEA agent you were palling around with?"

"He went to Mexico City. I guess they recalled him or something. I didn't really ask. Glad to be rid of him," Ernie said and gave Baker a thumb's up. "Seen Grace lately?"

"Not recently. I did see her once or twice. I think she got bored being in Mexico and hopped a plane to Paris or Rome. I forget where she said she was going."

"Oh, nice. I'll need to give her a call later," Ernie said.

"She left her phone here. Good luck trying to talk to her."

Ernie smiled. It meant Grace was with Cuba, and they were working together. It meant his best friend and his daughter were now working against him.

"Let me know a place you want to have lunch," Cuba said. "We can work it out. It will be good to see you again."

"Yes, it definitely will." Ernie disconnected the call and handed his phone back to Maria.

"What did any of that prove?" Maria asked.

Ernie grinned. "A lot, actually. He hasn't found the treasure. Grace is working with him. He's still in town. He wants to meet with me and agreed to it so quickly because he's out of options. He's obviously been diving a lot at supposed treasure places but at this point he has no clue what to do next."

Maria didn't look like she was as sure as Ernie. "You and Cuba meeting might end in one of you dying. Are you good with that?"

Ernie shrugged. "I'm good with living to count my part of the treasure."

SIXTEEN

"Nobody knows where this fucking treasure is," Grace said.

She'd finally been able to get Alberto and Rick together. They were sitting in the library of Cuba's house. The only place Grace was sure Cuba would never willingly walk into.

Grace wondered why he'd even rented such a massive place when the original plan was to come down to Mexico, get what they were looking for, and go back to The States.

It's like once they got a taste of living in luxury, the thought of staying in a normal house was horrifying.

Not that Grace couldn't understand that. All she knew since being born were designer clothes, nannies, not having to lift a finger to do anything. Hungry? Have the family's private chef cook something up. Need your hair done, a pedicure, a manicure? Bring the spa to the house.

Her father – a word Grace still thought of when she thought of Ernie – made sure that she didn't have to worry about anything. Whatever she wanted was hers. Grace didn't even have to ask. She had a card with no limit and never saw a bill.

She figured having an entourage of highly weaponized mercenaries with him justified the big place.

Better for Cuba and his crew, and even better for Grace and her plan.

"Isn't Cuba going to get suspicious that the three of us are suddenly hanging around together, alone in the library?" Alberto asked.

"Cuba is never not going to be suspicious, but this isn't going to ping on his radar more than a tiny blip. What else does he expect the people he's trapped here to do? Isolate ourselves? There's nothing suspicious about us having a drink together here." Grace looked around. "Except maybe for Rick being around books."

Rick looked up from the carved chair arms he was running his fingers through – a mouse trying to figure its way out of a maze – and gave Grace the finger.

"I went to fucking Harvard. Why is everyone giving me shit in my life lately?" Rick asked.

"Life in general seems to be giving you shit, my *hermano*," Alberto said.

"Ok, let's not start a pity party. There's nothing more annoying than two grown men blaming everything except themselves for how their life turned out." Grace finished her drink and walked over to the caddy to refill her glass.

"So are you both clear on what needs to be done?" Grace asked.

Rick and Alberto glanced at each other and then back to Grace.

"That's what we wanted to talk with you about," Alberto said. "We both have a feeling you're giving each of us just pieces of the plan. Rick brought up parts that you hadn't told me about. Same on my end. If we're in, we're going to need to know the entire plan. Not be compartmentalized. It doesn't gain a lot of trust when you're holding back."

"Kind of makes me think you're using us just to fuck us over in the end. Like father, like daughter, right?" Rick asked.

Grace poured the drink down her throat and slammed the glass on the table. She walked over to the bookshelves and started studying the titles.

"You're both paranoid. Do you really think I give a shit about the money? I have more than enough. And I'm not like either of my fathers. They both are addicted to the chase, to accumulating more and more wealth even though they'll never get through it in their lifetimes."

Grace pulled a book out that was backwards, glanced at the spine and sniffed, placing it back the correct way.

"It's not about the money for me. It's about doing everything I can to make sure Cuba doesn't get his hands on it. And if you want me to be honest, I don't particularly give a shit about either of you and where you end up in all of this. I just know that we all need each other right now. Maybe for different reasons, but we can still help. And, unlike Cuba, I have no intention of putting a bullet in the back of your heads when this is done. I mean, Rick, you seem like a decent enough guy. Although you're beginning to stink and need to shower. Alberto, same with you. Not the stinking part."

Grace moved to the next bookshelf and ran her finger across the dusty spines.

"Have these people not heard of alphabetical order?" Grace asked.

"Look, let's stop beating around the bush. Tell us everything, while we still don't have any unwanted company here," Alberto said.

"In time," Grace said, moving on to the last bookcase. She pulled a book and smirked. "Treasure Island. If only it was that easy, right? Robinson Crusoe is a bitch." She placed the book back.

Alberto stood up and finished his drink. "If you're just going to be a pain in the ass about this, I'm leaving. There's no point sitting in this stuffy room when I'm hungry and tired."

Alberto headed toward the door.

"Sit, Alberto," Grace said. "There's a reason for everything, and patience is the only way you'll get your answers. Also, even though I swept the room earlier, I can't be one hundred percent sure there aren't bugs in here."

Grace stopped and grinned, pulling two books from the shelf.

"Now what are the chances of having two of them here?" She mumbled.

"My electronic jammer should block any bugs, if there are any. So we should be good, but I still prefer not to say much aloud."

Alberto looked at where Grace pointed and saw a little small box with a wired switch hanging next to it.

"Where'd you get a bug jammer?"

"I made it. It's amazing what you can put together from random household shit. If you know what you're looking for."

Grace handed one of the books to Rick. "Here you go, Harvard. Read that. After you shower." She handed the other to Alberto, who reluctantly came forward and took it.

"The Count of Monte Cristo?" What am I supposed to do with this?" Alberto asked.

"Read it. Like I said. Pay attention specifically to the prison scenes. You'll enjoy it anyway. It's a fun book."

"It's a delicious sandwich, too," Rick said, paging through the book.

"That's a Monte Crisco," Alberto said, shaking his head at Rick and looking at Grace as if she couldn't believe that idiot.

Grace had no desire to correct Alberto. The two of them exhausted her enough.

"Just read the book. You can skim over most of the bullshit. The jailbreak is what's important. Read it like you need to give a book report in class. Which you basically will have to."

"This book is huge," Rick said.

"Do you have anything else to do? Besides Cuba's annoying outings to continue to not find any treasure? Read it. Don't try to hide it. We're being held captive by people who think books are used for fixing wobbly tables. Nobody will think anything of it. They may call you a nerd, though."

Grace left the two of them in the library while she headed upstairs to her room and the en suite bathroom to soak for an hour before she went to sleep.

Of course she was going to tell them both the full plan. But Grace was going to make sure she confused them enough that they'd be left at the end of it wondering just what in the hell she'd pulled on them.

SEVENTEEN

Arturo watched Ignacio as he walked to the bodega, wanting to attack his former friend but knowing he must remain calm. Ignacio knew something, he was sure.

Before he'd taken over the crew, Arturo had made sure to get as much information out of Ignacio as he could, being extra friendly and asking a lot of questions.

In the end, he hadn't learned much. He knew Ignacio had a good deal with the Americans but they'd disappeared. Arturo wasn't sure where they'd gone or what Ignacio was working on with them.

Leo was also gone, and that one was upsetting. He'd been watching Ignacio's home and was supposed to report back but he never did. It was impossible Leo had run off. Maybe something bad had happened to his second-in-command.

Catalina was nearby, waiting for further instructions. Even though Arturo had told the crew she was off-limits and his girl, he knew she wasn't interested in being his girlfriend. She liked the action and being part of the gang but that was about it.

Arturo was going to send her to Ignacio for information about Leo's whereabouts.

He knew he needed to do something and soon, because he could feel the eyes of the other kids on him now. The rush of initial power was exciting. It got his manhood hard, but then it had shrunk with the stress of keeping everyone happy and focused.

There needed to be a job for them to do, but Arturo wasn't completely sure how Ignacio had gotten them in the past. He hadn't paid enough attention. He'd never made direct contacts like the former leader, comfortable to do what needed to be done and not much more.

Now Arturo was paying for his laziness.

Catalina was staring at Arturo. He knew she was annoyed because she'd wanted to go and hang out with a few of her friends on the beach tonight, but Arturo had told her he had a special assignment.

"Is it messing with Ignacio? Why don't we leave him alone and try to do some of the exciting things he used to do with us?" Catalina had asked.

Arturo was mad she'd said it but knew she was right. So far, since taking the leadership role, they hadn't made any money. Ignacio used to find out when the tourists were arriving and getting teams together to pickpocket and confuse them.

He'd also know which bicycles and mopeds and motorbikes could be stolen and not come back to haunt them. Arturo didn't know how he did it, but they never got caught.

Some items they'd hold for ransom and get a few dollars for the safe return. Other times they'd sell them immediately and make money.

Arturo wasn't bringing in any money, which made him useless to the others. He knew it was only a matter of time before they'd turn on him. Take away his power and cast him aside like he'd done to Ignacio.

He waved Catalina over and she practically ran to his side.

"I need you to go and talk to Ignacio. Apologize for setting him up and try to get some information from him."

Catalina frowned. "So, you want me to set him up again? Like he won't know what I'm doing. He's smart." Catalina hesitated but then clicked her tongue. "Smarter than you, Arturo. If he knows anything, why would he tell me? He knows I'm not on his side any longer. He knows you're running things. Trying to, anyway."

"What does that mean?"

Catalina threw up her hands. "It means some people are talking. You haven't earned anything for any of us. Some of the crew are beginning to talk about doing their own things. Maybe reforming with someone else to lead them, like Leo."

"Where is Leo?" Now Arturo thought Leo was hiding somewhere, away from him. Working to gain the trust of the crew and take it over, right underneath Arturo.

"No one has seen him in a few hours," Catalina said. She was frowning again. "They said you sent him out all night to follow Ignacio in case he left or did something. What do you think Ignacio is going to do when he knows he's being watched every second of the day? Standing on this corner means we're not making any money. This isn't working."

"It is working and it will work... as soon as you get some information from him," Arturo said.

Catalina looked like she was going to walk away, but instead she threw up her arms again and started walking toward the bodega. "Stay out of sight. I'll meet you around the corner soon."

Arturo wanted to watch her in action but decided it would be ruined if Ignacio spotted him, so he took a walk around the block and sat under a broken street light several houses away, barely in sight of the bodega.

He knew he was running out of time. Arturo was also sure Ignacio had been planning something big before he was injured. Was he still working an angle, or had it all fallen apart when the crew had abandoned him?

Maybe I should have let him stay in command but undercut everything he did, learned what he was planning and then swooped in and taken it from him, Arturo thought.

Too late to wonder what if now, though.

Catalina and Ignacio walked out of the bodega together and they were smiling.

Arturo took it for a good sign. He shrunk back into the shadows when Ignacio started to look around. He had to know he was being watched.

Would he fall for Catalina being nice to him? Arturo hoped so.

Catalina was definitely being flirty. She kept twirling her hair and then touching Ignacio's arm. Ignacio didn't seem to hate it. He was grinning.

After a few minutes, Ignacio gave Catalina a big hug. He had a bag of groceries in his hand and he walked down the block toward his home.

Arturo waited a full minute before stepping out and waving to Catalina, who joined him on the sidewalk.

"Well? What did he say? What did you get from him?" Arturo asked.

Catalina shook her head. "Not much. He's not stupid, like I said. He knows you sent me to talk to him. He was very vague about everything. We talked about the upcoming football matches and how our families are doing. Not much more."

Arturo groaned. "You were supposed to get information from him."

"Like what? Should I have asked him where we could make some money? How do all of his scams work? If he has a hidden treasure chest under his bed, filled with Mayan gold and artifacts? Be serious. You blew this."

Arturo was mad. He clenched his fist, although he would never hit a woman. Only cowards did that. His father, before he'd fallen drunkenly off of the roof, had beaten Arturo's mother every few days.

"Keep at it. He will slip eventually and give you some real information," Arturo said.

"Like what? Tell me what you want from him and I can try to work on it."

Arturo had no clue what Ignacio was hiding, but he wanted to find out before it was too late.

EIGHTEEN

"So then what?" Agent See asked. "You pretend to be one of Patek's men to get me down here and then think you're going to put pressure on me to go against him?"

George laughed and turned sideways on the seat, his arms resting on top. He had to admit, this was a nicer SUV than Ernie had ever sent for him.

"Shit, Mr. Santiago. Or Diego. Can I call you Diego? Of course I can. Diego, you could have just gotten in contact with me and been open about your... problem. What was the point in trying to fool me?"

"We weren't sure how loose your moral connection to the Agency was. There are tons of agents out there on the dole in some manner. Most deal with pussies like Patek. They will not come near the Cartel." Diego Santiago grabbed a bottle of water from the cooler and handed it to George.

"Of course they won't. Thank you, I'm parched." George took his time drinking half the bottle, purposely ignoring Diego and looking out the side and back windows at the scenery as he was being brought to whatever compound the cartel had. "Not many of us want to get involved with your people. Survival rate and all that."

"But you are fine with the risks involved?"

"For the right amount of money, I'm fine with most everything. And considering Patek doesn't actually need me for anything, I don't want to waste a trip down here without making some profit. Tell me about what happened to your brother. Because Baker sure as shit couldn't kill a cartel enforcer."

Diego told George what he knew. George had a feeling it wasn't much, and most of it was guess work. His brother was found dead on the beach after being seen in the company of the cartel's local head, Maria Guerrero, Ernie Patek, and Baker Cioffi.

Multiple witnesses saw Maria do the actual killing, but Diego seemed to be convinced that Ernie and Baker had a part in it, whether by blackmailing Maria with something, or all three teaming up.

George didn't know why Diego assumed Maria didn't act alone. To him, it was pretty clear. Sure, Ernie would be involved with the cartel, and probably had gotten involved in something that he was now running from. But Ernie getting the drop on a cartel head and having her off her second-in-command? Didn't seem likely. And Baker... George wasn't going to waste time trying to put that together. Baker almost definitely fell ass backwards into the current situation.

No. Maria acted alone. He was sure of that. But if Diego wanted to convince himself that Ernie Patek had a part in the killing, and wanted him in, then George had no problem with that as long as the money was right. Sure, he'd be losing a stream of side income by giving Ernie up, but he'd potentially be gaining a more lucrative one with the cartel.

George glanced out the back window of the SUV and waited for Diego to finish his story. The details no longer mattered. The choices were simple: backstabbing Ernie and Baker, and handing them over, or probably being brought to the desert and being set on fire or having his limbs cut off with a chainsaw after refusing. It was a no-brainer. George enjoyed being alive.

George turned to face Diego after taking another look at the traffic behind them.

"Why?" He asked Diego.

"Why what?"

"Why not just find the two of them yourself and do whatever it is you have planned?"

"Optics. There are still people in the cartel who have dealings with Ernie Patek. People who wouldn't be happy with what I want. At least not until they close out their accounts with him. If someone else is seen with them last, it takes the heat off of me. They might suspect, but they wouldn't know. Usually suspicion is all you need to lose your head in this business, but luckily I'm high up enough to warrant a bit of proof before a hit is put out."

"And Maria? What do you have planned for her? She is the one who actually killed your brother. Maybe it would be easier to focus on her."

Diego shook his head. "She may have, but she couldn't have done it on her own. Someone must have forced her to. Ernie and your rogue agent Baker must have forced her hand. She wouldn't kill Raul on her own."

"Why not?"

"Raul's my brother. Her second-in-command. We've all known each other since we were kids. I know her and she wouldn't have done it without being under some kind of force."

George finished his water and dropped the empty bottle on the floor of the car. He watched Diego make a face at the move, the first sign of emotion he'd seen from him since he'd been... what? Kidnapped? Or at least forcefully held for the moment.

"Maybe Raul was going for her position. Setting up a coup."

Diego's annoyance grew. George smiled, knowing this guy, however dangerous, was easy to anger and therefore easy to manipulate. If you couldn't control your emotions, any of them, you left yourself open to a smarter person's use.

"I'm not here to hash out possibilities. I want Ernie and Baker brought to me and I want you to do it so it doesn't come back on me. And forget about Maria. She was blackmailed. End of story."

"Ok," George said, leaning back in the seat. "Just one more question and I'll be out of your hair. That is, if you'll let me go once we shake on this. We've dealt with this section of the cartel before. I've heard Maria Guerrero's name. I've read her file. Now, I don't have an eidetic memory or anything, but from what I can recall, her life seems pretty buttoned up and secure. You're talking blackmail. Let's forget about the fact that Ernie can be a bumbling mess and Baker is so incompetent that he actually misspelled his last name once on a field report. If they blackmailed Maria into killing Raul, I can't think of anything I've read about her that they'd be able to dangle in front of her."

"She has a child. They must have threatened her kid. She would do anything for the boy, so they must have found that out somehow and used it against her."

"I don't remember anything about a kid in her file."

"It's a closely guarded secret. You can count the number of people who know on one hand, even if I cut off a couple fingers."

"And how do you know?"

Diego leaned forward, close enough that George could smell the scotch on his breath. A little early to be drinking. Another fault George could use to his advantage in the future.

"I am the boy's father. Raul is his uncle. Now you see, don't you? I know Maria. She would never kill my brother. She's a crafty bitch, but I can see through her like glass."

"Well, I don't get involved with family issues, so let's leave that alone. I'll get you Ernie. I can guarantee you that. But I need to deal with Baker on my own. You want me to do your work because you need to be shielded from your higher ups. I need to take care of Baker for the same reason. And, trust me, just because he's somehow tied in with Patek doesn't mean he did anything but shit his pants around Maria and Raul. He's not the man you want."

Diego contemplated this, and nodded his head. He put out his hand.

"Get me Ernie, you can do what you want to your agent."

George shook his hand and sighed.

"Just one more issue. Something we're going to need to figure out sooner rather than later."

"What's that?"

George glanced behind him again. "You have a tail. Been following us since we left the airport. Two men. Two American men. Two very annoying, yet very talented, agency men. They must have seen me in the airport. Benford and Tally."

"I'll have my men take care of them."

"You'd better hope so. Those are two agents you don't want on your ass. This agreement of ours has not started out with good luck."

Diego didn't seem to understand the gravity of the situation. He just shrugged and grinned.

"You know what the saying is," Diego said. "If it wasn't for bad luck..."

"Your brother wouldn't be dead?"

Diego's face betrayed his emotions once more.

George sat back and smiled. He'd give up Ernie. Then, he'd see what he could use this imbecile for.

NINETEEN

Cuba surprised Rick by barging into the room and motioning for Rick to follow him.

Lucky I wasn't pleasuring myself or trying to get with JoJo, Rick thought.

With nothing better to do at the moment, Rick followed Cuba out of the villa to a waiting car, glad when he got inside the air conditioning was cranked.

"Where are we going? A donut run?" Rick asked.

It was only him and Cuba, with one of Cuba's men driving.

"We're on the same side now, Rick. Working together for a common cause, which is making us rich. I think it's time we pooled our resources together and moved this along," Cuba said.

"Meaning what?"

Cuba smiled. "You have boots on the ground in Mexico. You've been able to tap into a vast network of street urchins, and they give you information. We need to use them again, not only to find the treasure but to see who the other players are in this game."

"It's not really a game at this point. Way more life and death," Rick said.

"Tell my driver where to go to meet one of your contacts."

Rick took a second before giving the driver a street name. There was no exact address to meet with Nacho. The boy was usually floating around somewhere, but he'd always seem to know when Rick was looking for him.

"Are you worried about other players? Ernie and Baker resurfaced? Maria?" Rick asked. He needed information flowing his way, too. This couldn't be a one-way street of information if this was truly going to work.

Rick also worried Cuba was going to steal JoJo and kill him, too, but one problem at a time.

"I'm worried about a lot of things. In my line of work, there are no coincidences, there are no friends. There is only hardship and enemies around every corner. It keeps you on your toes. It keeps you safe." Cuba shook his head. "Sometimes I think you aren't taking any of this seriously. Why do you think that is?"

Rick smiled. "Now you want to play shrink with me? Not interested. You worry about you, Cuba, and I'll worry about me. There's nothing that matters except the job at hand."

Cuba shrugged but didn't say another word until they'd arrived on the block Rick had said to drive to.

"Now what?" The driver turned his head and looked at Rick.

"Now I take a walk," Rick said and opened the car door, feeling the heat rush inside.

"I'll go with you." Cuba opened his door.

"Not a chance. They don't know you. Actually, they definitely know you and who you are and what you've done, so you stay with the car. I need to find Nacho. Alone." Rick got out and slammed the door. He walked half a block before glancing back, smiling that Cuba hadn't decided to follow him.

Rick took his time, glancing into stores and cafes, as if he was a simple tourist window-shopping.

He saw a couple of kids but they were with their parents. He knew not all children worked for someone like Nacho, but all he needed to find was one of them.

Rick smiled when he saw a girl staring at him. He recognized her as one of Nacho's crew.

"Hungry? I'm going to get a couple of tacos at the corner," Rick said as he passed her by.

She fell in line behind him.

Rick ordered four tacos and two cold sodas, sitting down on a nearby bench. The girl stood nearby but didn't sit, although she thanked him for the food and drink.

"I'm looking for Nacho," Rick said. "I have some work for him."

The girl was about to bite a taco but stopped. "He is no longer in charge."

Rick frowned. "What?"

"Arturo is our new boss," she said and took a bite of taco.

"I don't know him."

She finished her first taco before answering. "He was Ignacio's second. He took over the group and runs things now. We all work for him."

Rick shook his head. "Then I will find someone else to help me."

"No... please. Arturo can do whatever you need. We might not have Ignacio but we have the same group as before. I am Catalina. I will be your go-between," she said.

"Well, Catalina, here's the thing... this is all very sensitive. I trust Ignacio with it, not someone I've never met or who I might've met but he didn't register for me. Understand? I need information in real time, which Nacho could always give me," Rick said.

"Arturo can do it, too. He learned a lot from Ignacio."

Rick ate his tacos and finished his soda. "What happened to Nacho... and do not lie to me."

Catalina turned her head and Rick thought she looked sad.

"Is he dead?" Rick didn't know the kid too well, but he'd immediately grown fond of Nacho. He didn't want anything to happen to him.

"No. He was injured. Badly. He recovered, but by then it was too late. Arturo took over the group and we all went with it. What else could we do? We didn't know if Ignacio would be back to lead us again." Catalina sighed. "He is still alive and getting stronger, but it's too late for him. Arturo will never let Ignacio gain control again."

Rick didn't want to interfere with any of this, but it was gnawing at him. If Arturo was as good, even half as good, as Ignacio, he could be valuable.

Plus, I can hand Arturo to Cuba as the contact and get in touch with Nacho and see what I can do to help him, Rick thought.

"I need the address for where Nacho is," Rick said.

Catalina gave it to him, only a couple of blocks away.

"We need to meet Arturo. Today. In an hour. Right here. Can you do that, Catalina?"

She nodded.

Rick smiled at her. "Then I will see you again and hopefully we'll work together." He walked away and headed back to the vehicle, getting back inside and welcoming the cold air.

"Well?" Cuba asked.

"I was down at the corner, near the taco stand. Arturo is the leader of the group of street kids. He will meet with us in an hour," Rick said.

"Perfect. Then we need to kill some time and watch for his approach," Cuba said.

"Yeah, that sounds like a lot of fun. Not. I have a personal task to attend to, but I'll be back in plenty of time," Rick said and opened the door again.

Cuba grabbed Rick by the arm.

Rick pushed the hand away. "If you don't trust me then we can't really be partners in this, right? I handed you my street contact without question. Cut me a damn break. I have something to do and it won't take long."

"Is this about drugs?" Cuba asked.

Rick was annoyed at the question. Everyone still thought he was using. He wondered if Cuba had been a little bird in JoJo's ear about it. Maybe to hasten her breaking up with Rick and being with Cuba.

"Fuck you," Rick said before he got out and slammed the door again.

TWENTY

The ride back was longer than Ernie expected. It was also bumpier, and by the time he saw the town come into view, his ass felt like he'd been hit by a bull a couple dozen times.

Nobody said being on the wrong side of the law was easy, but Ernie expected at least some comforts considering the amount of money he'd built in.

Maria hadn't wanted to take a chauffeured car back, saying something about it being too obvious. But Ernie tried to push back, talking about tinted windows hiding two gringos and a pretty Mexican woman from sight. It was simple logic. Ernie was also thinking about the minibar that accompanied most fancy SUVs, and the usual snacks that went along with it.

Apparently, Maria didn't appreciate the finer aspects of life and instead insisted on stealing a car and swapping plates. She said that would give them enough time to get out of Mexico City and back to the Pacific coast.

At least she could have picked something besides this rust bucket, Ernie thought.

Ernie looked over his shoulder at Baker, who seemed to be having just as rough a time in the back seat. At one point during the ride, Baker had actually asked if they were there yet, like an eight-year-old. Maria had shot him a look that almost cracked the rearview mirror and Baker hadn't said a word since.

"Hey buddy. Buddy Baker. How you doing back there? You hungry? I bet you are." Ernie turned to Maria, who was focused on the road. He could see the muscles in her jaw clench and unclench. Obviously she knew what was coming, but Ernie didn't care. "Maria, you think we can stop once we get into town for a snack? Baker is starving. I bet he'd like some of those delicious taquito things from a street cart. Hell, we wouldn't even have to get out of the car."

"No," Maria said, giving Ernie a look and then focusing back on the road.

Ernie sighed. They'd had to stop for gas, but Maria hadn't let either of them out of the car any of those times. And even though he'd pointed out multiple places along the way where they could grab a quick bite, she refused. Ernie figured she had to eat at some point during the long trip, but the bitch must have a reserve stomach or something.

Between the heat – because she'd not only picked a rust bucket, but a rust bucket with no A/C – and the lack of food in his stomach, Ernie felt faint. Even though they were approaching the town, he didn't know if he'd live to cross its border. He was probably hallucinating it anyway. What kind of animal doesn't let two grown men stop and get lunch?

Maria grabbed her hat from the center console and put it on, pulled it down close to her eyes. She gestured at Ernie and Baker.

Ernie rolled his eyes and put on the I Love Mexico City hat she'd bought him, while Baker donned his Yo Quiero Taco Bell cap.

"These aren't going to do anything but make us more suspicious," Ernie said.

"It's better than nothing, so please shut up about it. I had to hear complaining the entire trip. I'd like to end it in relative silence."

"I'd like to end it with a fucking quesadilla," Ernie said under his breath.

"What?"

"Nothing."

"How much further? Because all this jostling about makes me have to take a shit," Baker said.

"Don't you start, either," Maria said. "We're close. Just please, for the love of God, both of you shut it."

Ernie gave a sigh of relief as Maria drove into town. They were finally back to some form of civilization. The trip had been a lot of scenery of nothing, which made him uneasy. He was in his element around people, even if they were strangers. Being in the middle of nowhere was torture.

"I still don't understand why it was the best idea to come back here," Baker said from the back.

"Because it's the last place the cartel will think to look for us. All three of us left in a hurry. Why would we come back here just as fast?"

"That's what I was asking," Baker said.

"No, I mean... Never mind. We're here. If you can't trust me, at least believe me when I say this is the best plan."

"Where are we going, anyway? We can't stay at one of your places. I'm pretty sure anybody you try to rent a room from is going to know who you are," Ernie said.

"Don't worry about it. I have a place."

Maria took them through a couple turns and into a section of the town Ernie didn't recognize. Not that that was a difficult thing to do. Since he got here, he'd spend almost all of his time at the beach hotel, the beach bar, or the upscale restaurant, surprisingly, on the beach.

It looked like an area he wouldn't want to find himself in, anyway. Some place where he'd send Cuba if he had some business to conduct.

The thought of Cuba both enraged and depressed Ernie. It made him think of Grace and what she was doing. If she was alright. Ernie knew his daughter, as he still, and always would, think of her, and she was more than capable of taking care of herself. Cuba may be a thug, and a smart one, but Grace was more cunning than anyone Ernie knew. He'd been aware of some of the things she'd done, but he was sure that the only reason he ever found out was because she wasn't trying to hide it from him.

Maria stopped in the middle of a narrow side street. Ernie looked around at the garbage on the street and swept up against the side of the buildings. Nothing here was over two stories. The sun beat down on everything, fading any colors that had once been painted.

A group of kids ran across the street, kicking cans. A scraggly dog followed after them, barking at their heels.

"You expect me to stay here? You want me to get mugged?"

"Nobody is getting mugged. Calm down."

"I'll calm down when I get some food. Is there going to be food at this safehouse of yours?" Ernie asked.

Maria shook her head and got out of the car. Baker and Ernie stood up and stretched. Ernie felt all the bumps and dips, sharp turns and backfires as his back cracked.

They followed her around a corner and down an alley to a small wooden gate with peeling paint and into a small backyard. Some clothes hung, drying on a line. A couple chickens wandered around the dead grass, pecking at grain.

Ernie wondered if they'd be able to grab one of those and fry it up.

"Where are we? Who lives here?" Baker asked.

"My sister. We'll be okay here. I'm not saying she'll be happy about it, but we'll be fine here for now."

"You have a sister?" Ernie asked.

"Why is that shocking to you?"

"I don't know. I just figured the Ice Queen wouldn't have any relatives."

"Ice Queen? What do you mean?"

"You know, the Ice Queen. From... never mind. Let's just get inside and hope your sister's got some grub."

They walked in, Maria in the lead, to a conversation. She stopped for a minute before continuing into the main part of the house.

"Who's this?" Ernie asked.

"This is my son, Ignacio. This man, though, I haven't had the pleasure of meeting. Though I do believe you were with my son on the boat that exploded and helped him after he was shot. For that, I'll let you live long enough to explain why you are here, Mr..."

The man stood up, giving Ernie a weird look.

"Rick. My name is Rick, and my girl JoJo is the one who stole your map, Mr. Patek."

TWENTY-ONE

Talk about awkwardness. This is going to be interesting and an added wrinkle in all of this, Rick thought.

He'd ditched Cuba and his man and found the address of Nacho, knocking on the door and asking his mother if he was home.

"Mister Rick? Is that you?" Nacho smiled and told his mother it was fine, to give them some privacy and could she please get them both a refreshing drink?

Once they were alone in his bedroom, Rick leaned against the wall and glanced out the window. He saw the girl, Catalina, with another girl, across the street. "What's happened, Nacho? Who is Arturo and should I be worried, for you and for me?"

Nacho groaned but quickly told Rick what had happened when it came to Arturo and him taking over.

"Then we'll get it back for you," Rick said. "I have a meeting with Arturo in less than an hour. Cuba wants to meet with him and get his help, but I'd rather have you leading the group."

"I'm not interested," Nacho said, but it was obvious to Rick the boy had had his feelings hurt and was trying to act like he didn't care. He most certainly cared about being ousted.

Rick smiled when Nacho's mother entered the room and handed them both a cold drink. The woman kept glancing at her son, trying to get his attention. Likely to ask who this grown man, this gringo, was and why he was in her home and in private with her young son.

"I will explain all to you in a bit, mother," Nacho said. "In the meantime, my friend Rick said he has some money for you. To thank you for your hospitality."

Rick smiled and took out his wallet, handing over half of the cash he had. As soon as the woman took it and left, Rick had to laugh. "Very nice move, Nacho. I did not see that coming."

"She'll leave us alone now," Nacho said. "If you were trouble in any way, we have code words I would have said. Then she'd get some of the neighbors and they'd beat you to death."

"Oh, very pleasant," Rick said. He pointed out the window. "Why are they watching you? I spoke with Catalina. She told me where you lived."

Nacho smiled faintly. "What else did she say?"

Ahh, he has a thing for Catalina. Good to know. Hopefully we can fix all of this and not ruin the kid's relationship with her, Rick thought. "She passed me a note in homeroom and said she liked you."

"Homeroom? Huh?"

Rick waved his hand. "Never mind. A bad joke. Let's worry about getting you back in charge, because I have a feeling Arturo can't do as good a job as you've done for me so far. There's a lot at stake, too."

"Like what?" Nacho asked.

Rick frowned. How much should he tell this kid? "A lot."

"Tell me or I won't work with you. I swear," Nacho said.

"Fine. But... oh, shit, kid. We've been searching for a shipwreck and treasure, which you probably already know," Rick said. "Actually, I don't really even know what you know. Everything happened so fast out on the water."

Nacho nodded. "And you think I know where this treasure is?"

"No, but I think with your system in place you'll be able to help us locate it. So far we've been diving on half a dozen spots but with no luck. The hope is that one of your crew will be able to hear a rumor about the location," Rick said.

They were interrupted by the door opening and Maria, Ernie and Baker stepping inside the small bedroom.

Ernie pointed at Nacho and asked who he was.

Maria smiled. "This is my son, Ignacio. This man, though, I haven't had the pleasure of meeting. Though I do believe you were with my son on the boat that exploded and helped him after he was shot. For that, I'll let you live long enough to explain why you are here, Mr..."

Rick didn't know how to react to any of this. He was glad he was alone with Nacho, and Cuba wasn't here, either. That could lead to some real problems.

"Rick. My name is Rick, and my girl JoJo is the one who stole your map, Mr. Patek."

Ernie groaned. "You have a son?"

Maria looked confused. "Son? No, no, I said nephew." She put her hands on Nacho's shoulders. "My sister's child, Ignacio. You misheard me."

"I heard you say son, too." Baker was staring at Rick. "What did you hear?"

Rick nodded. "Definitely said son. We all heard it."

"Freudian slip... is that the term?" Maria bent down and hugged Nacho. "He is like my son. A growing man of the house. I am very proud of everything he does." She stood. "Why are you alone with my *nephew*?"

Rick sighed. This was not going to end well. He had a really bad feeling about this scene unfolding. "It's a private matter. I came here to ask for some help with information, which your *nephew* could help me with."

"Nothing is private when it comes to my family, so tell me what the situation is," Maria said.

"Look, we're all after the same thing. A sunken treasure. I was going to have Nacho and his crew gather information around town, so maybe we can find it." Rick wondered if he'd survive jumping out the second-story window, if need be.

"His name is Ignacio, not Nacho. That is a bad nickname and I've never heard him called that. Ever," Maria said. She turned back to Ignacio. "Is this true? Are you running with a gang?"

Nacho pumped up his tiny chest and raised his head high. "I was their leader, until Arturo took over while I was in hospital. Mister Rick was going to help me get my crew back, too."

Maria shook her head. "Give me the information on this Arturo, and I will deal with him."

Ernie cleared his throat. "What are we going to do now? I'm hungry."

"I'm supposed to meet with Arturo in about fifteen minutes." Rick sighed. "Along with Cuba, who is the one who actually wants to hire the street kids."

"That sonofabitch," Ernie said. "Where is Grace?"

"She's back at the villa, with JoJo and Alberto. Cuba and one of his men will be looking for me, and I need to get back to them and meet with Arturo," Rick said.

Maria pointed at Rick. "Tell me where this meeting will take place and then go to it."

Rick told her, not knowing if this was a good thing to do but not seeing how any of this could get any worse than it was right now.

"Tell no one you saw us, especially Cuba. We'll be in touch with you soon enough," Maria said and moved aside so Rick could pass.

Rick didn't know whether to trust her but saw an opening and rushed out of the home and back onto the street. It was even hotter, the sun directly overhead and scorching his skin and the pavement.

Now what should I do? Maybe I could trust Maria, Ernie and Baker, long enough to get the treasure and get rid of Cuba once and for all, Rick thought.

He strolled down the street, wiping the sweat from his face. Wondering what was going to happen next.

TWENTY-TWO

Even though Cuba was gone, Grace didn't want to take a chance on escape. Her father would just find her again, and who knows what he would do at that point? Would she become such a problem that he would kill his own daughter?

Despite what she'd told Alberto and Rick, she wasn't very concerned for her life. They were definitely in danger, but she was fairly sure that Cuba wouldn't kill her, despite what he may say. Hurt her? Of course. However, because she wasn't one-hundred-percent positive her life wasn't on the line, she was going to go through with the plan. An escape attempt now would just mean more eyes on her after she was caught.

What concerned her now was Cuba taking off with Rick. No word of where they were going. Would he come back alone, leaving Rick's corpse behind? There was no doubt in Grace's mind that Rick for sure wasn't pulling through this hunt. Not as long as he was an obstacle between Cuba and JoJo. But it was too early to get rid of Rick.

As much as she didn't like it, Grace put herself in her father's shoes. No, Rick would be coming back. It wouldn't make sense to kill him now. Which means Cuba was off doing something with him that he didn't want the rest of them to know. At least not for now.

She propped up the pillows on the daybed in her room and turned off the movie she'd just started a few minutes ago. Some bullshit with Liam Neeson and a kidnapped daughter. Why watch the movie when she was living it in real life?

Grace put on something brainless for background noise and opened the *Treasure Island* book she'd taken from the library. She had read it when she was younger, but apparently Ernie had bought her some kind of abridged version, since this was much more detailed. It didn't surprise her. Ernie, if he had to read at all, was more of a Cliff Notes kind of guy.

Someone knocked on her door. Grace rolled her eyes and sat up, telling the person to enter. Either her father was back, or one of his guards was pretending to have something to tell her when he was really just trying to flirt. Although, she'd be surprised if that was the case, considering the hammer punch she had delivered to the balls of the last guard who'd tried that.

The door opened and Alberto came in. He closed it behind him and stared at the knob for a moment.

"You have a lock on your door? Shit. I don't even get a doorknob."

Grace shrugged. "I guess being the kid of the guy who's holding you captive has its perks. What do you want? I'm busy trying to do anything but deal with people."

Alberto sat and lifted the copy of *The Count of Monte Cristo* he held in his hand.

"I don't get it," he said.

"What don't you get? How to open a book? See what you do is, you put it so the words are all facing the right way–"

"No, *pendeja*. You told me and Rick to read this. To pay attention to the jail parts. I don't get what you're trying to say. I also don't know why you just won't come right out and tell us what the entire fucking plan is. It's like you don't even know."

"You read that entire book? Don't bullshit me."

"No, I didn't read the entire book. I skipped over anything that didn't have to do with the prisoner. Boring ass book. Why would I read parts I'm not supposed to focus on anyway?"

"Tell me what you got out of it? Sum it up for me, Al."

"Guy gets thrown in jail. He escapes."

"How does he escape?"

"Dig a tunnel with some priest."

"That's not how he gets out of jail. Read it again."

"Jesus, Grace, can you just come out with it already?"

"The priest dies before they can finish the tunnel. Dantes escapes prison by switching places with the dead body. He gets dumped over the prison wall and into the sea."

"Great. Thanks for the clarification. I still have no idea how this pertains to what you have planned. Find a dead priest? Get tossed overboard?"

"It's not meant to be literal. Dantes escapes because the jailors think they are seeing something they aren't seeing. They're also too lazy to do their jobs properly. Why bury a body when you can just toss it over the wall? They think that's an easy solution. Assholes in charge of other people tend to go for the path of least resistance. They also tend to overlook something right in front of their faces."

Alberto tossed the book into the air and leaned back on the daybed. The book hit the floor, its back cover facing up.

"I give up. You talk too much like a crazy person who doesn't make sense. Jailors. Bodybags. Switcheroos. Hollywood bullshit. Maybe just do what you need to do and I'll do what I need to do."

"Alberto, stop stressing and think about it for a second. There's no way I'm just going to come right out and say it. I don't know if this place is bugged or not. I do know my father's not stupid enough to think I wouldn't try to plan an escape, preferably with the treasure, so I don't mind talking about it in general. Just take a moment to think about what I told you and what I asked you to do. Put it all together."

As she spoke, Grace handed Alberto *Treasure Island*, opening it up to page five and pointing to a word she had circled. He looked confused, but got the point that she was trying to show him something without anybody who was listening in knowing about it.

Grace flipped a few pages further ahead and pointed at another circled word. Alberto nodded, grabbing the book from her and flipping through the pages, turning the circled words into sentences.

Alberto dropped the book next to the other one on the floor and stared at her.

"There's no way that can–"

Grace put a finger up to his lips. She pointed to him and then rapped him on the head.

Alberto sat for a few moments. Grace could almost see the pieces slowly coming together for him.

"Got it?" She asked after a few more minutes.

Alberto nodded again.

"Like I said, maybe you should do your own thing. I'll do mine. You're a... you're a crazy person." Alberto gave her a thumbs up as he was talking and walking toward her door.

Grace rolled her eyes. They couldn't all be great actors. At least she'd thoroughly swept the room for cameras.

Alberto left and Grace grabbed both books off the floor. Sometimes she found dealing with the mentally inferior extremely frustrating. But she guessed if she was going to make it in the world, she would have to learn to handle it.

She left the room, after tearing out and flushing the pages with the circled words, and replaced the books back onto their shelves in the library.

When she turned around to head back, JoJo was standing a few feet away from her. Grace, startled, jumped back and almost took down the shelves.

JoJo walked up to her, put her arm on her forearm and began walking her back to her room.

"Now that your scumbag father isn't here to interrupt, I want to know what the hell you and Alberto have planned with Rick."

Grace felt her stomach drop. Part of the plan hinged around JoJo not knowing about it.

She was really starting to not like this woman.

TWENTY-THREE

Rick met up with Cuba and his driver and they went to the spot to meet Arturo. Cuba didn't say a word but he looked annoyed.

He really wants to ask me where I went but his pride won't allow it, Rick thought.

A kid he assumed was Arturo was standing next to the taco stand. Rick noticed a few more hanging around up and down the block, and glimpsed at least one more on the roof of the building across the street. With so many people coming and going, they could hide in plain sight.

Rick's FBI training kicked in, and he placed everyone in a grid on the street in his mind's eye, so he could keep track of who was a player and who was a nobody. It cut down on the chaos and calmed him, too.

"Are you Arturo?" Rick asked, since Cuba was still silent.

"Si." He offered a hand, which Rick shook. "I heard you were looking for information. I can provide whatever you need."

"Let's hope so." Rick pointed at Cuba. "This silent, handsome bastard is Cuba. I guess he's in charge of things. Maybe he'll even speak."

Cuba gave Rick a dirty look. He seemed distracted and Rick now noticed he kept looking around. "Is there a more private place we can go and conduct business?"

Arturo frowned. "No. We do this on the street, in view of many people. I don't even know you."

Rick smiled. He knew Nacho would've weighed the pros and cons and found a private spot he'd already set up for a meeting. He'd done it the first time Rick and JoJo had met with him, letting the other party think they were making the decisions.

Arturo is not smart enough to run this crew, Rick thought.

Cuba was still looking around. "There are too many ears. I don't like this. Maybe I will find someone else to do this important work for me. Thank you for your time."

"No, wait." Arturo was also looking around. He'd obviously set up a perimeter like Nacho would've done, but there was no plan B for it. No thought of the meeting being moved to another location. "Give me a minute and I will find us a secure location."

Cuba was now staring at Rick as Arturo ran across the street and began conferring with another street urchin.

"Have you eaten?" Cuba asked Rick.

"A couple of tacos. You?"

Cuba shook his head. He took money from his pocket and handed it to his driver. "Get us some tacos. I would like scallop tacos if they are available. But keep me in your sight in case this little brat decides to do something foolish."

Rick knew Maria was going to be around, somewhere. He hoped Arturo's crew didn't spot her. He was also worried she might do something stupid like appear with a butcher knife and try to stab Cuba or something along those lines.

Arturo returned. Rick noticed the kid he'd been talking to run off.

"Give me a second and we will have somewhere to go," Arturo said. He stared at the tacos as the driver came back over.

"You want one?" Cuba asked.

"Si, sir."

Cuba doled out the tacos and Rick didn't get one.

I'm fine. I already ate. Jokes on you, idiot, Rick thought. He would've eaten a couple more but he'd have plenty of time later to have all the damn tacos he wanted.

They all stood around on the corner eating tacos, except for Rick, until two boys waved at Arturo and motioned for the group to follow.

"No funny stuff, kid, or I will not only kill you and your entire crew but also anyone even remotely related to you," Cuba said. He smiled. "And since we're in Mexico I guess I'll be killing nearly everyone we see."

Arturo looked more confused than scared as he followed the two boys two blocks to an open cafe that was currently closed. The patio area out back overlooked the ocean as it dropped down a small hill through small trees and dirt patches.

Rick noticed a couple of goats wandering between the cafe and the ocean. If it wasn't for being with Cuba and talking to a little punk that had taken Nacho's crew away, this would be pleasant. He wished JoJo was here, and thought maybe when all was said and done they could come back to this spot and enjoy some strong coffee.

Cuba and Arturo sat across from one another at a table, Rick preferring to stand nearby. The driver posted up at the only entrance to the patio area, hand on his weapon at his side.

"Tell me what you will need and I will name my price," Arturo said.

Rick was sure he'd heard Nacho negotiate this way many times.

How do I get rid of this kid? I need Nacho back in charge. He's the only one that might be able to actually find something, Rick thought.

"I'm looking for a sunken treasure," Cuba said to Arturo.

"Off of the coast?"

Rick chuckled. "No, buried in someone's backyard. Do you know what the word sunken means?"

Cuba put up a hand to silence Rick. "Obviously, this is very important. We need to find it. I will cut you in for a share, of course. Depending on if you can help to locate it and how much help you give us. Understand?"

Arturo seemed to be thinking. "Do we get any money upfront? I will need to gather the information and it will not be cheap. If there is a treasure out there..." He glanced at Rick. "In the ocean, I will find it. But it will cost me, which means it will cost you."

Cuba took out a crisp one hundred dollar bill. "Ever seen one of these?"

Rick thought Arturo was going to faint. A hundred was equivalent to a week's worth of high wages in Mexico. Roughly two thousand pesos.

Cuba put the money on the table and added two more. "Will this be enough for you to start?"

"Si, sir, yes, yes," Arturo said, snatching the money and putting it in his pocket.

Rick caught a glimpse of the child in Arturo, and wondered what he would be like if he wasn't in the streets hustling. It was a shame what these kids had to endure and–

The shot rang out, nearby, and everyone scattered. Rick hit the ground and saw blood. He panicked thinking he'd been hit.

No, it was Arturo. He wasn't dead but he had been hit in the arm. The bullet had exited his body and Rick knew he'd live. Who was shooting?

Cuba had stumbled out of the cafe and thrown himself down the hill. Rick thought he also might have been shot.

The driver had returned fire but was then killed by a hail of bullets a second later.

Rick was still trying to process the number of shots, number of gunmen, if he was about to die.

Maria stepped into the cafe and groaned. She rushed to see if she could shoot Cuba but he'd already disappeared below, scaring off the goats.

"You will come with us," Maria said to Rick.

"No. I can't leave JoJo with Cuba. I need to run and act like you were trying to kill both of us," Rick said. "I will pass you information if anything happens." He turned to Arturo. "He stole your son's crew."

"Ignacio is my nephew," Marisa said. She still had the weapon in her hand. "Nephew."

"Sorry. Yes, your nephew's crew." Rick bent down to Arturo, who was moaning on the ground, trying to stop the bleeding. "Give up the crew to Nacho."

"No," Arturo shouted.

Rick stood. "Then no one will call for an ambulance. You will die."

"No." Arturo moaned again.

"No, what?" Rick asked.

"I will do it. He can have it back. I'm not good at this, anyway. Too stressful, gringo."

Rick nodded. He turned to Maria. "I need to run away and act like you're chasing me. I don't even think Cuba saw it was you trying to kill him, so I will let him know it was a couple of random thugs trying to rob us."

"That will work," Maria said. She put the gun to Rick's chest. "Do not cross me or I will end you and JoJo. Understand?"

"Si, ma'am," Rick said and ran off.

TWENTY-FOUR

Nigel adjusted his seat belt and glanced at Mike. The windows to the SUV they were following were tinted black enough that only occasionally, if the sun hit them right, he was able to make out the shadow of a person inside. But that didn't mean they couldn't see them, and that was his concern at the moment.

"Did you even go through training, or do you have a relative who pulled some strings and got you into the agency?" Nigel asked.

"What the hell are you talking about?"

"Tailing a car. I'm just assuming you don't want to be so far up its ass they can taste our exhaust. But what do I know, right?"

"You're talking to me about how to follow a suspect? Remember Rio? I doubt you could forget that incident."

"Different situation. And I told you not to bring that up again."

Nigel turned up the air conditioning and hit the recirculate button. Mexico. Brazil. That three month stint in St. Augustine. Why couldn't he ever be sent to a nice, temperate climate? Always with these hot zones. Maybe the heat caused higher incidents of crimes. He knew he was definitely close to a homicidal mood.

"What are we doing following Agent See, anyway? We're supposed to be tracking down Patek and Cioffi. Who cares what that sociopath does?" Mike asked.

"The dude's sketchy. If he's down here he's not involved in anything good. And what are the chances it doesn't have something to do with Patek?"

The SUV turned off the airport road and headed down a side street. Mike followed, backing off a bit. It was the only admission Nigel would get that Mike took his advice to leave some space between them.

"You know about this guy, right? Agent See? He might be a sociopath, but I've heard some stories. They say he's like the DEA James Bond. All kinds of licenses to do whatever he wants. Untouchable. That type of thing." Mike followed as the SUV made another turn onto an even worse backroad.

"Rumors. He probably started them himself."

"I don't know, they say he was the one who took out the dude in Bulgaria. Clean sweep. Nobody even knew he was there."

"Exactly. Nobody knew anybody was there. Which means he can swoop in and take the credit around the fucking water cooler and the actual guy who did it isn't going to say anything. He's a blowhard. I'd be surprised if he ever drew his gun in the field."

The SUV turned again, leading them further out from the city. Nigel wasn't sure where Agent See was having the driver take him, but as far as he was aware, Patek and Cioffi were still in

Mexico City. Unless intelligence hasn't updated them yet. Nigel checked his satellite phone just in case. No new messages.

"Something's strange here," Nigel said.

"What?"

"I don't know. Where the hell is he going? And how'd he get a nice car and a driver? We had to rent this boxy piece of crap car. Rent it and then wait to get reimbursed."

"I told you. James Bond, man."

"No, something is going on. There's no way he's here on agency business. Or he's doing some side hustle on the DEA's time."

Nigel pulled up the map on his GPS and zoomed out to see where they were compared to Mexico City. The map showed a dotted line from the airport to their current position. They'd headed straight out of the city toward the east, then began to circle the outskirts of the city.

The SUV made a couple more turns, before breaking from the loop it had been making and headed south.

"He knows we're following him," Nigel said.

"How can you tell?"

"Besides your subpar driving techniques? He's having the driver circle. Buying time. Or leading us around like morons. They just broke pattern and are heading south now. I don't like this."

"Let's drop him and go do what we were sent here to do. I've been saying this all along."

Nigel shook his head. "If he knows we're tailing him, he'll stop to talk. He might be a loose cannon, but he's not going to try to take down two other agents."

A few minutes later, the car turned off road and led them into a valley that hid them from any traffic that might pass by. Nigel sat in the car, waiting for Agent See to make the first move.

The back door to the SUV opened, and George stepped out. Mike opened his door and got out before Nigel could stop him. He cursed and got out as well.

"Well this is a surprise," George said. "What are the chances of us meeting like this? You two out on assignment?"

"Unfortunately. Would rather be home in some air conditioning. But you gotta go where the job takes you, right?" Nigel hated the small talk that usually happened when he met a fellow agent in the field. He'd rather get down to what they both really wanted to know and go on their way.

"What do they have you doing out here, See?" Mike asked.

"Oh, nothing really. I'm not actually out here on agency business. Freelancing is more like it."

Nigel unbuttoned his suit jacket and moved his hand next to the gun holster on his waist. He knew George would notice, but didn't really care. Better to alert the other guy and be ready than get caught with a gun in his face.

Something wasn't sitting right with him, and George just bluntly acknowledging he was rogue meant that Nigel's initial thought that they wouldn't be in any mortal danger may have been wrong.

As Nigel was about to say something, the door on the other side of the SUV opened and a tall, built man in a very expensive suit stepped out. Nigel immediately unholstered his weapon, but kept it at his side. Mike did the same.

Three black vehicles pulled in behind them. Half a dozen men got out, weapons pointed at Nigel and Mike. He looked over at George, who motioned for him to put his gun down.

"Patek and Cioffi are mine to deal with. I'm assuming that's why you're here also." George took a few steps toward them and a gun appeared in his hand faster than Nigel could register it. Maybe the rumors Mike had been talking about were true.

"Guns down, agents. Don't try to buy time, you obviously have no choice."

"What are you going to do, See? Shoot us? You'll be on the run forever. Every agency in the country will be looking for you," Mike said, tossing his gun to the ground.

"I'm not going to kill you, Mike. Calm down. I just wanted to give you the message to stay away from Patek. Hang out in Mexico City for a while. Enjoy the food, the women, then go back home and report that you hit a dead-end."

Nigel took a deep breath and looked at Mike. They could agree and say that was what they were going to do, but George knew that would never happen. They were in a mess they couldn't get out of, and unless the literal hand of God came down and saved them, they would never be going back to The States.

He wouldn't be able to take out the cartel men, but at least he could get a shot off at George and take the bastard with him.

As if reading his mind, George lifted his weapon and fired at Nigel, hitting him in the shoulder. His gun dropped to the ground.

Mike dove for his and Nigel watched as a few dozen bullets from the cartel guns peppered his body.

When everything was silent again, George shook his head. "Should have taken them out."

"There never was an out, man. Just get it over with. Make it fast if you have any sense of decency."

George looked at the other man who had exited the SUV. The man gestured to his cartel crew and then both of them got back into the car and pulled away.

Nigel closed his eyes as the first of the bullets were fired.

TWENTY-FIVE

Cuba wasn't sure who had tried to kill him, and there were too many variables to work through as he tried to stay alive and get back to the villa.

It might have been the cartel, or Ernie, or maybe Rick had set him up, or Arturo for some reason, or the local police or the Feds or DEA or... there were a lot of people who would be happy to see him eliminated.

He didn't want to use his phone to get a taxi or call Grace or JoJo because he was now paranoid he was being watched. His phone might be tapped.

Cuba kept glancing at the blue sky overhead, afraid to see a helicopter or a drone monitoring his every move. He didn't see anything and heard nothing, but that didn't mean they weren't up there.

The streets were crowded, which could be a good thing. He'd be able to blend in.

Or if I'm being followed or there's a killer ahead of me, they could easily bump into me as I walk and shank my gut, Cuba thought.

He took his time moving, trying hard not to get too close to anyone.

At the next corner he stopped and leaned against a building, looking around to see if he was being followed. He couldn't tell, because the crowds were always so chaotic.

He was on the move again, and as he passed a stand where an older woman was selling braided hats, he managed to scoop her phone off of the table in front of her.

Cuba called JoJo, who didn't answer. He kept trying until she finally answered.

"Why didn't you answer when I called?" Cuba asked, hearing the anger in his voice. He was on the verge of a breakdown, and he needed to remember his military training. His breathing exercises. He needed to center his chi.

"I didn't recognize the number," JoJo said. "You sound out of breath."

"Well, so would you if you were on the run. Someone tried to kill me."

"Who? Where's Rick? Why did you two run off? Where are you now?" JoJo asked, rapid-fire.

"I'll give you a street corner and I'll need you to tell one of my men to pick me up," Cuba said.

"I'll give one of them the phone. They won't believe me. Hold on and let me go find one of them."

Cuba kept walking in the general direction he needed to go, knowing if he stayed on the street too long his would-be assassin or assassins would find him.

"Here's one of your men," JoJo said and handed over the phone.

Cuba got to a corner and told the man what the cross streets were, and told him to hurry and make sure he had backup and was well-armed.

JoJo got back on the phone. "He's running off. Who tried to kill you?"

"I'm not sure. Pick an enemy at this point. It could've been a robbery gone bad. Your guess is as good as mine." Cuba didn't like standing in one place, waiting for his ride, but he knew better than to rush off and not get picked up. "As for Rick... I don't know where he is or if he's even still alive."

Truth be told, Cuba hoped Rick had been shot and was dead. Even though he might need the man to find the treasure, he was a pain in the ass and in Cuba's way to get JoJo. With Rick gone, maybe it would be smooth sailing.

Based on how this day was turning out, though, Rick was still alive and might have been part of the assassination attempt.

"I need to call Rick," JoJo said. "I'll see you back here soon."

"JoJo, don't let Grace know. I don't need her worrying." Cuba wanted to say more but she disconnected.

Cuba tried to get as close to a building as he could, put his back to it and prayed to a God he didn't believe in to protect him. He knew the cartels all had their South American god they worshiped, one who would supposedly save them from arrest or death.

La Santa Muerte. Saint Death. Cuba thought that was the name of the god.

Maybe I need to start praying to it, too. Can't hurt, Cuba thought.

A man was coming down the street and he looked angry. Cuba braced himself for an attack but the man breezed past him and started yelling at a woman on the next corner.

Within a couple of long minutes, the SUV pulled up and one of his men got out, brandishing an automatic weapon.

"Out that away," Cuba said through gritted teeth as he climbed into the vehicle. "We don't want to give anyone a show."

Cuba felt better but couldn't be completely relaxed until they pulled into the villa compound and the gate was closed. He rushed inside and called out for Grace.

She was by the pool working on her tan and a mojito.

"JoJo told me you got attacked. That sucks," Grace said and took a sip of her drink. "Can you ask one of these idiots to get me another one, and make it stronger?"

Cuba didn't know what he'd expected from Grace. Her being scared for him, wondering if he'd been shot? She didn't seem like she even cared.

She's just like her damn mother. A sociopath. Selfish. Only cares for herself, Cuba thought.

Without a word he went back inside and swore he wasn't going to be bossed around by his daughter and get her another drink. "JoJo? I'm back. Where are you?"

He swept through the lower floor, calling out to her.

When he got upstairs he rushed to her room, hoping she'd be more receptive to his return. Maybe she'd been worried sick about him, maybe now that he was back and safe, he could turn this into a positive with JoJo.

She might give him a hug. Maybe they'd stare at one another before kissing. Maybe an embrace would be enough.

Cuba knocked on her door and tried to look like he'd been through a rough couple of hours, trying to project he'd need a long hug from her.

"JoJo? Are you in there? I've returned."

"Come in," JoJo yelled.

Cuba opened the door and stepped inside.

JoJo was seated on the edge of the bed, smiling at him.

"Wait until you hear about the day I've had so far," Cuba said and moved toward her.

He saw movement to his right and turned.

"I see you made it back alive," Rick said, seated in a chair near the open door to the deck. "Thanks for trying to save or find me."

Cuba shook his head. "There was so much confusion. Gunshots, blood. I think the little boy was killed. I thought you were right behind me, but it was one of the goats following. I was going to send a team of men to find you. I swear."

Rick shook his head. "I don't believe you, but so be it. We still have a lot of work to do."

"Did you see who tried to kill me?" Cuba asked.

"Kill *us*... and no, I did not. I was trying to run for my life, too." Rick stood. "I need a stiff drink."

TWENTY-SIX

Baker finished his third bowl of stew and leaned back in his seat, holding his stomach like he was nine months pregnant. It had been spicy as hell, but he was so hungry he didn't care. Besides, the overhead fan hitting the sweat pouring down his face felt as close to air conditioning as it appeared he was going to get in this new hellhole Maria had brought them to.

Ernie was gesturing with his empty bowl to Ignacio's mother, or aunt, or whoever the hell she was. He wondered if Maria had really misspoke, or if the little shit really was her son. That sort of information would get him a ton of brownie points with the DEA. As far as anyone knew, Maria had no connections with anyone outside of the cartel.

The woman reluctantly refilled Ernie's bowl, at least his fourth, and walked off muttering something in Spanish that didn't sound complimentary.

Baker looked around the house, if it could be called that. He tried not to be judgmental in his normal life, but after all the crap he'd been through, his tolerance for most things in life was very thin.

He guessed the place wasn't too bad, considering the area. The floor was nicely tiled and clean, and there were a couple hallways leading off into other sections he hadn't seen yet. From the outside, Baker would have thought it was a one room shack where everyone slept on thin mats on the floor.

His eyes circled around, moving up and down the walls and ceiling, taking in the place, until they landed on Nacho, who was staring directly at him and scowling.

"Hey. 'Sup?" Baker asked, a little put off by the stare he was receiving.

"You eat like a pig, American. Do you know how hard I work to make sure we don't go hungry here? And you put down more stew than an elephant."

"Is that how you talk to guests here?"

"You're not my guests. My aunt brings you in and leaves you here, then expects us to feed you. Well, you're fed. You can leave now." Nacho pushed back his chair and carried the empty bowls and utensils to the sink.

"Got any chips?" Baker asked. He smirked, knowing the question would get under the kid's skin.

Nacho turned and flung a bowl at Baker's head. Baker ducked just in time, and the bowl smashed against the wall behind him.

"Jesus Christ, kid, I was just–" Baker stopped speaking. He tended to do that when he had a gun pointed at him. The kid had just reached into a drawer like it was nothing and pulled the damn thing out.

Ernie looked up from his stew and chuckled before going back to slurping the food down.

"You get nothing else," Nacho yelled, the gun pointed steady at Baker's face. "No more stew. No chips. No carnitas, no tacos, no goat. No... no... no Twankies."

"Twankies?" Baker frowned, despite the very real possibility that he might have to deal with a bullet lodged in his skull.

"Little yellow, cum-filled dicks you Americans like so much."

"Oh. Twinkies."

"You got Twinkies?" Ernie asked through a mouthful of meat.

"Shut the fuck up, man. Kid's got a gun pointed at me."

Nacho put the gun back in the drawer and slammed it shut. Baker still didn't like the look he was giving him, but a look couldn't blow brains out of your head.

"Why are you two here anyway? And with Aunt Maria? You don't look like her normal companions."

"We just have some business to take care of. Then we'll be out of here."

"But why do you have to stay here? Stay at a tourist hotel."

Baker debated on how much to tell the kid. "We're just trying to stay out of sight for now. Some people might be looking for us."

Nacho nodded. "Cartel. I'm looking at two dead gringos."

"Look, buddy. We'll be out of your hair soon. For now, let's all play nice," Ernie said. Baker could tell he wanted yet another refill, but seemed to be gauging whether asking would set Nacho over the edge.

"I'm not your buddy. And I'm done playing nice. Every time I try to do something to help someone, I get screwed. Fucking shot. Fucking de-throned. My streets taken from me. But that's all going to change soon. Mr. Rick is going to help take care of things. You two, though? You can't help me, so you're both useless and just taking up space."

"Sounds like you've got some issues to work through," Ernie said.

Nacho opened his mouth, probably to say something nasty. Baker really was shocked at how much of a dick the kid was. But before he could say anything, the back door opened, and Maria walked into the kitchen, weapon at her side.

She sat at the table and placed the gun on it. Baker could feel the heat radiating off it. Wherever she had been, the gun wasn't used just for show.

"Where the hell have you been?" Ernie asked. "Your son-nephew has been berating us like he's the next fucking Pablo Escobar."

"Pablo Escobar was Colombian," Maria said. She looked at Nacho. "Your friend Arturo has been injured. Someone shot him accidentally. He's off to hospital. He made it clear that he doesn't have the cojones to be leading a pack of street urchins and he'd be happy for you to relieve him of that duty."

Nacho jumped up, looking excited. He ran out of the room and came back in a moment later in a new change of clothes. He grabbed a different gun from another drawer and stuffed it down the front of his pants.

"You know, you really shouldn't carry it like that," Baker said.

"Shut up, stew hog. I'm back. I've got my crew back. Time to get back in business." Nacho went over to Maria and kissed her on the cheek. "That's for whoever accidentally shot Arturo."

Nacho left the house. Baker looked at Ernie and they both looked at Maria.

"Did you shoot a child?" Ernie asked.

"No, I didn't shoot a fucking child." Maria wiped the sweat off her forehead. "I mean, yes I shot a child, but not on purpose. That bastard Cuba was in town. I had followed Rick and thought I'd got a good bead on the fucker's head. He moved at the last second and the bullet hit the kid."

"What happened with Cuba and Rick?" Baker asked.

"Cuba ran. Rick and I spoke quickly. He's not with Cuba. He's being forced to dive. To search for the treasure, but he wants out. We can use him to take care of Cuba and get the treasure."

"What about his wife, or girlfriend, or whoever? And Grace? And whoever else Cuba has held hostage," Ernie asked.

"One thing at a time. We have Rick, who can tell us about where they're staying and help us infiltrate and take out Cuba and his men."

"The three of us? I don't know if you know this, but I spend most of my time at the DEA sitting at a desk and writing reports. Actually, mainly pretending to write reports while I play Minecraft on my phone."

"No, not you. Not you either, Ernie. You two stay behind. I have some people I can call. I can't use my old crew as most of them were more loyal to Raul than me. But I knew a few people who would be more than happy to jump in this just to be able to kill people."

Maria walked out of the kitchen and into one of the other rooms. Ernie stood and walked to the oven.

"Are you eating again?" Baker asked.

"That's not a pertinent question. The real question is why aren't you?"

TWENTY-SEVEN

JoJo joined Grace at the pool, knowing Cuba and Rick were going to both be watching them carefully. There were a lot of things now in motion.

Rick had come to her after the attack and laid it on thick about what a coward Cuba was for running away without firing back, how he'd left Rick to die, and how the only reason they had a meeting with the kid was because of Rick's connections.

After Cuba had come into her room, surprised to see Rick alive and having beat him to her, JoJo saw the dynamic between the men for what it was: they were both making a play for her.

Not that she wasn't flattered by the attention. JoJo felt like it had been too long since any man had been so attracted to her he might kill for her affection. It was great for her ego and it gave her drive and purpose.

"I need to know what you're planning," JoJo said to Grace without looking at the girl.

"You don't need to know anything, even if I was planning anything. You're so wrapped around Cuba's finger." Grace started to get up to leave but JoJo put a hand on her arm.

"Stay. We need to talk. Woman to woman. We hold the power here, not those two," JoJo said.

Grace frowned but she sat back down and put her head up toward the sun. "Fine. I will need another mojito soon, though."

"I flirted with one of the idiots working for Cuba. He's making us a pitcher of margaritas." JoJo laughed. "Again... you and I hold the power. Not Cuba or Rick or any other man in the villa."

Grace sat quietly, never turning to look at JoJo.

"If we work together–"

Grace sighed. "There is no we. I'm not sure what Rick told you but there is no plan. There is no grand scheme that I put together. Only the need to find the treasure, split it equally and never see any of you people again."

"As if any of this was going to be that simple." JoJo stopped talking when the man came out with a pitcher of margarita and three glasses, as if he was going to join them.

JoJo smiled at the man and handed him the third cup. "We'll only need two, but thank you. I really appreciate you making this. I'm sure it will be fantastic."

She watched as he slumped his shoulders and walked off, looking pitiful. She still had that effect on men, even if she sensed he was more interested in trying to get Grace drunk and make a move.

Sure he was gone and not lingering near the door, JoJo poured them both a glass and handed one to Grace.

"How does it feel to be you?" Grace asked.

"What do you mean?"

Grace shrugged her shoulders. "Past your prime. Once something that every man might want but now a bit long in the tooth. A shell of your former self. I imagine it gets lonely only being able to impress a man like Rick or a man like Cuba. I'm going to guess when you were my age you had some really interesting men who would do your bidding."

JoJo forced herself to smile. *I'm not going to let this little skinny bitch get under my skin. She's trying to manipulate me,* she thought.

"I'm not looking forward to being as old as you," Grace said. "Hoping I die before I get old, like the song."

"You're not nearly as young as you think you are. It will catch up to you soon enough, which will be good for you, Grace. You have wide hips, excellent for bearing children to some loser who thinks he hit the jackpot by knocking you up, thinking you're a pain in the ass and a royal bitch but at least your family has money. Especially if we find this treasure and you actually get a cut of it," JoJo said.

Grace didn't look pissed. In fact, she started to laugh and took a sip of the margarita. "This is good. Keep that guy around. He needs to make me drinks from now on."

"Tell me the plan," JoJo said.

"In time. Right now there are things in motion. I won't shut you out but I don't trust you. I'm sure you understand why." Grace took another sip and smacked her lips. "So good."

"I want what you want," JoJo finally said. "What's coming to me. What I deserve. I am also like you because I don't care about anyone else."

"That is a true statement. It doesn't matter if Ernie or Cuba is my biological father, it doesn't matter who's trying to be nice, it doesn't matter that Rick keeps making passes at me... I only care about myself," Grace said.

JoJo didn't know if Rick had actually made a pass at her or if she was saying it to get a wedge going between JoJo and Rick. For now she decided to push it off to the side and not dwell on it.

"Well, whatever it is you have planned, I hope it works and you aren't an asshole and shut me out, because I've done nothing to you," JoJo said.

Grace finally turned and looked at JoJo. "I never said you did anything to me."

"Then what is your problem?"

Grace grinned. "Maybe I'm afraid I'll grow old and look and act like you. Maybe you are my worst fear. Or... maybe I have nothing against you at all."

JoJo wanted to punch her in the face but grinned back.

"I'm just glad when I was your age I was at least twice as smart as you think you are. There is a world out there, the real world, where a skinny little bitch like you is a nobody. Where no one will give you a second look, and guess what? It's all downhill from here for you," JoJo said.

Now Grace was smiling broadly. "Thank you."

"For?"

"Calling me skinny," Grace said.

JoJo shook her head. "I didn't mean it as a compliment."

"Yet, that's how I took it. So thank you." Grace finished her margarita and poured herself another one from the pitcher.

JoJo wanted to keep pushing Grace, but knew the girl was in a foul mood and would only keep saying nasty things.

"Enjoy the rest of that," JoJo said and stood.

"Oh, I will. Run back to Rick or Cuba and fill them in on what we talked about." Grace was no longer looking at JoJo. "I might go for a quick dip in the pool."

I hope you drown, JoJo thought.

She went back inside the villa, hoping neither Rick nor Cuba were going to want to talk to her. She needed some privacy and some space for a while.

TWENTY-EIGHT

It wasn't difficult for Alberto to get permission to leave the house. At least, not once Cuba came back.

He'd try to get one of the guards to let him out, explaining the situation. But they were all idiots who didn't understand half of what he was saying. Most of them had never been in water deeper than their bathtubs. Some, by the smell of them, hadn't even been in that much.

Alberto had been waiting for Cuba to get back, listening for his entrance, but it turned out he could have been completely oblivious and still would have known Cuba was back.

He'd busted through the door like a bull, making a bee-line toward JoJo's room.

Alberto had cut him off.

"I need to go to the dock."

"No," Cuba said and tried moving around him. Alberto stepped in front of him again.

"We're going out tomorrow morning, yes? So, I need to run through a checklist on the boat. It's procedure. Top off the tank, and all that."

"You can do that in the morning when we're all there."

"Yes, Cuba. You are absolutely correct. But you've seen how long that takes. It would be better for all of us if I did it today. We could push off as soon as we board. I'd also be able to run through the checklist without all the distractions that come from everyone else hovering around."

Cuba looked toward JoJo's door, then back at Alberto. He walked over to the sliding glass doors and yanked them open.

"Go with Alberto. Make sure he does what he needs to do and bring him back," Cuba said to the guard outside.

It's like the man can foil a plan without even knowing there's one to foil, Alberto thought.

"That's not going to work," Alberto said. The guard stopped and looked at Cuba.

Cuba turned to him.

"Why not? Because he won't let you start the boat and drive away into the ocean?"

"Why would I try to escape? And to where? I make my living in this town. Outside of it, I'm nobody. Not to mention the cut of the treasure you promised. That would go a long way toward my retirement."

"If I let you go, you go with a guard or you stay here and we deal with it tomorrow."

I really hate this guy, Alberto thought.

"I bring him, people ask questions. This time of day, there's going to be a lot of people around. At the bar. On the beach getting ready for bonfires. Most of the boats will be coming in and docking. It's not like when we go at dawn. Even if he gets rid of his gun and dresses like a normal person and not like a G.I. Joe reject, the people there will sniff him out. But it is important this gets done. Last time we went out we were close. I could feel it, couldn't you? The extra hour it took to launch in the morning could have gone toward finding the treasure. Just let me go before the sun drops. Even if I did try to run, it's not like you wouldn't be able to find me."

Alberto took a small GPS out of his pocket. They hadn't confiscated it when he was brought to the house because it couldn't do more than just show location. It didn't broadcast its own coordinates and there was no option to send any emergency call or signal. Alberto just had it to be able to make sure his boat was always where he left it. Too many thieves around.

He could track the boat and disable it if he saw it was being moved.

He handed the GPS to Cuba.

"Now you have full control. That will beep and vibrate if the boat moves more than ten feet. This button here will disable the engine and steering."

Cuba stared daggers into Alberto's eyes, then snatched the GPS from his hand.

"Two hours and you're back here. Any longer, I send two men to gut you and I find someone else to pilot the boat. Now get out of my way. Some shit went down today that I need to deal with."

Alberto looked at his watch as he finished the safety checks on his boat. He'd rushed through it since he was only given two hours, which included travel back and forth. The shitty scooter he was given to get to the docks didn't go over thirty miles per hour.

He had just under an hour and twenty minutes would be taken up with the drive back.

Alberto finished up and rinsed his hands in the salt water, splashing some on his face. He was shaking and needed to calm himself down. While the chances of him being seen by someone who would get word back to Cuba was slim, there was always a chance he'd sent someone to secretly keep an eye on him.

Alberto had been pretty careful to make sure he wasn't followed, but it's not like they didn't know where the damn boat was. Maybe Cuba had someone watching it around the clock.

Scanning the area for anyone who looked suspicious, Alberto walked across the sand to the bar.

It was starting to fill up. He hadn't been lying about the beach getting crowded toward dusk. It was a good thing. The more people around, the less he would be remembered.

He walked into the crowd to the bar counter and ordered two beers. As he sipped one, he scanned the bar and was on the brink of an anxiety attack when he finally saw him. He wasn't sitting in his usual chair, but he was just as drunk as always.

Alberto walked over and put the sealed beer in front of the man slumping over the small hi-top table.

"Christian. How have you been, amigo?"

The man seemed to snap out of his stupor immediately, as if shocked, and looked at Alberto.

"Hey, man. Good. Good. It's been a while. Is this mine?" He pointed at the beer. Alberto gestured for him to have it.

"Yeah, I've been busy. Lots of charters. It's been a good year so far. How about you? Been out on the water a lot?"

Christian waved the comment away. "You know I can't take my boat out. The second I do, I'll be swarmed and arrested. As if it was my fault that person died. Do you know how many times I've taken charters out while I've been drinking and never had an issue?"

Christian continued to talk, but Alberto tuned it out. He'd heard the story many times, and it was always the same. The fact was, the guy was absolutely at fault for the death, and the authorities in town would not let him pilot a boat. Probably never again. Not in a town that relied on tourist money.

And they were not joking around about it, either. Alberto had found that out firsthand.

Christian had the same model boat as Alberto, and there had been a number of times the authorities had chased him thinking his boat was Christian's. Finally, Alberto had made some cosmetic changes in order to make his boat noticeably different. Getting stopped with a full complement of tourists on board wasn't good for his business.

For a long time, Alberto had been angry at the situation. He'd hoped Christian's boat sank at the dock, and had entertained the idea of scuttling it himself many times.

Now, with fifteen minutes left before he had to head back to his makeshift prison, Alberto was glad he hadn't followed through with sinking it. For the first time, he was happy to sit and listen to Christian explain away his negligence.

TWENTY-NINE

Ignacio was annoyed that none of his old crew was surprised he was back. In fact, they acted like nothing had ever changed. He'd always been here.

Catalina gave Ignacio a hug, which made him blush.

"Arturo is in hospital. They say he'll live but he won't be in any shape for a few weeks," one of the kids said.

"That was a shame what happened to him, whatever it was," Ignacio said. "No matter. We have work to do and we need to get to it if any of us want to get paid."

He knew this was going to be a wild goose chase, because he already knew where the treasure was. He was the one who'd found it, but he was worried someone else would stumble upon it at some point.

Moving it wasn't an option. Ignacio had no clue where to hide it or how to get it to any other location without being spotted.

While he wanted to trust Rick or his aunt, he knew that might not be a smart move. Not that he feared either of them stealing the wealth, but they might be watched. They might be dealing with ruthless people who wouldn't think twice about killing them and Ignacio.

Ignacio knew there were too many variables he didn't know and things his young mind might not be able to consider. It was too risky.

He hadn't even opened the chest and he was dying to do it, but a kid walking around town with a crowbar and hammer might seem too much for prying eyes.

Who could he trust? Ignacio had no clue.

After the shooting of Arturo, he didn't even know if Rick and Cuba were still interested in the crew working for them. Ignacio knew he'd need to assume he was. It would give the crew something to do, something to keep them in line, and also waste time while he had the treasure.

He seriously doubted there was another treasure somewhere out there they were looking for. No, he'd found it and he needed to keep it.

But it was too exposed. What if Cuba rented a plane to go up and down the coast? They'd spot it for sure. All it would take was a fishing boat too close to shore to see it.

If a local found the treasure it would become front page news. And whoever found it would be in danger, too. The cartel would never let them keep it, and Cuba, Ernie, Rick, etc. would also go for it.

Unless Ignacio was able to capitalize on the treasure and get it out of the town. Him and his mother could escape to a better life somewhere else. Maybe even in the United States.

Ignacio knew he couldn't do it alone, though. He'd need either Rick or Maria to help with all of that, which meant giving them a cut of the treasure.

Why am I not automatically giving it to Aunt Maria? She is family. She is blood, Ignacio thought.

He also had mixed feelings now because of what she'd said.

Maria had called Ignacio her son, not nephew, at first.

Ignacio wondered if it could be true. He'd always had his mother and her sister in his life as far back as he could remember. Maria had always given them money and taken care of them, and spent a lot of time with Ignacio when she was in town.

As he got older he realized what she did for a living. What she really did. His mother wanted nothing to do with all of that but reluctantly took a handout when it was absolutely needed.

Ignacio knew his mother had an idea what he did on the street but she would only offer some advice and not get too in his face about the path he was on.

He never used his aunt's name when dealing with anyone. He prided himself on being his own man, on figuring his own path and knew someday she'd be so impressed with his little empire he'd built she'd take him into the cartel as well, and he'd be a powerful leader.

Now he wondered who was his mother and who was his aunt.

Has his entire life been a lie?

Ignacio gave busy work to everyone in the crew, since standing around doing nothing wasn't making them any money. Menial tasks like finding the tourists and picking their pockets, breaking into hotel rooms and stealing wallets and jewelry, hanging out on the docks and getting whatever they could get.

"I'll see everyone back here in six hours, and you'd better have something to show for the time," Ignacio had said.

It felt good to be back in charge, to have tasks and a crew to command.

He decided to visit Arturo in hospital and get a feel for what the former friend was going to do once he was back out on the street. Would he now kowtow to Ignacio, or become a bigger enemy?

Ignacio wasn't going to wait around to see what happened. He needed an answer and needed it right now.

Instead of asking at the front desk of the hospital, Ignacio slipped in through a back door and wandered around, looking like a sad child so no one would bother him.

Within minutes he found Arturo's room and was glad he was alone. If his mother or any family was with him, Ignacio would keep walking.

Arturo had his eyes closed but Ignacio knew he wasn't sleeping.

"Hey. How are you feeling?" Ignacio asked as nicely as he could.

Arturo opened his eyes. "Weak, but I'll be stronger soon. Maybe a couple of days." He lifted his bandaged arm. "The bullet went right through. I was lucky."

"Yes, you definitely were. I heard there were many bullets in the air," Ignacio said.

Arturo nodded. "Are... why are you here?"

Ignacio could see the fear in Arturo's eyes. "I want to know what you plan to do once you get out. I've taken back my crew."

"Yes, I was told by your aunt to step down." Arturo licked his lips. "Is it true about her?"

Ignacio looked away, thinking word had already spread she might be his mother. "About what?"

"That your aunt works for the cartel."

Ignacio looked at Arturo. "Works for? No." He shook his head. "She is a leader of the cartel. I never wanted to use that for my own gain, but she is family. She will protect me, and she will strike down my enemies no matter the cost. No matter how young, too."

Arturo looked at his arm. "Was she there to kill me then?"

"I don't know. Maybe. You crossed me. You stole from me. You tried to undermine all that I've accomplished. Again... family." Ignacio wondered if Arturo was weak enough that he could put a pillow over his former friend's face and smother him to death.

A nurse came in and frowned at Ignacio. "Have you checked in at the nurse's station, young man?"

"I was just leaving," Ignacio said and pointed at Arturo. "I will see you on the streets. Think about what you want out of your future, because a big decision is going to come. An answer will be needed."

THIRTY

Grace laid on her back, taking in the sun rays and letting herself be calmed by the rocking of the boat.

Another day, another dive. It seemed like she was stuck in a big loop. She didn't help out in any way, and Cuba kept telling her she didn't need to come with them, but she enjoyed the sun and also needed to make sure she knew everything that was going on.

She caught one of the guards sneaking glimpses at her and gave him the finger.

Cuba initially had asked her to be part of the dive team. Although he wasn't there to raise her, he'd been around enough to know she was well-trained and probably the best diver out of all of them. Grace always refused and eventually he stopped asking.

She didn't know if he was maybe trying to form some kind of bond with her, to become the father he never was. But he didn't seem to realize that he would never be that parent. As much as she found Ernie abhorrent, she still considered him her real dad.

She wondered where Ernie was. What was he doing? He just fell off the map, which was strange for him. Grace thought he would have tried contacting her, or at least Cuba to find out what the hell he was doing. Maybe he had and she hadn't been told.

JoJo and Cuba were in the water, down at the bottom sucking sand off the ocean floor hoping to uncover something valuable. She was starting to believe there was no treasure. It wouldn't have been the first time Ernie had been taken with some grandiose scheme.

Rick looked overboard, leaning on the boat, trying to see through the murk of the kicked up sand. As if he thought Cuba and JoJo were heavy-petting through their wetsuits or something. He was too distracted with that shit. Grace was having serious doubts about bringing him in on the plan.

But she needed two other people, and she hadn't told him the full idea. She hadn't told anyone the full plan. Alberto knew most of it. At least, she thought he did. He seemed to have understood the message she'd circled out in the *Treasure Island* book.

She glanced at Alberto. He was sitting on his captain's chair staring out to the horizon. He must have felt her looking and turned her way. Grace raised an eyebrow and Alberto gave a slight nod.

She knew he'd been allowed to go to the boat yesterday afternoon. She hoped he'd done more than just the pre-launch checklist he claimed he was doing. For now, she'd have to take that little nod as if he'd started the plan rolling. Later tonight, when they were all back and exhausted, Grace would have to get him alone and confirm.

She heard a scrambling on the boat, and everyone moved to the side Cuba and JoJo had gone in the water. She sat up and saw bubbles rising to the surface. Shortly after, their heads emerged and Cuba spit out his regulator.

"We got something. Something big. Could be the rib of a boat. A couple feet under the sand."

"It's just a piece of wood. It's always just a piece of wood," Rick said after helping JoJo onto the boat.

"Definitely man-made," JoJo said. "I don't know if it means anything. If it's just a barren wreck or something tossed overboard at one point, but it's more than the nothing we've found so far. I think it's worth a look. Get your suit on. We need more help uncovering this."

Rick sighed and went to grab his suit.

Grace didn't know what was going on with him. He seemed strange ever since he and Cuba had been shot at. Could just be the shock of barely missing taking a bullet, but she didn't think so. There was something else there.

If Rick was hiding something from her, from all of them, she needed to either find out what it was or cut him out of the plan. Tell him some bullshit idea to make him think he was still involved, and let him run off in the wrong direction.

The three of them went back under, leaving Grace, Alberto, and two guards on the boat. Grace dipped a hand in the water and wet her body down, then stood and headed to the front of the boat.

The guards' heads turned as she passed them. She smiled. Stupid, horny men never paid any attention to anything other than a pair of tits or a nice ass. They definitely wouldn't bother listening to anything she spoke to Alberto about.

"What's stopping us from taking down those two men and just driving off?" Alberto asked, keeping his voice low and facing away from the guards.

"If we do, we leave behind any hope of treasure and a really pissed off Cuba. We'll be broke and have a price on our heads. Or at least you'll be broke. I'm assuming I still have my account. Unless Ernie got pinched by Feds and everything associated with him is frozen."

"Where is your father anyway? Ernie?"

"No idea. I'm sure he's fine. Cuba may have broken off from him, but Ernie eventually will put something together and take care of him."

Alberto stared into the distance, saying nothing. Grace glanced at the guards, who quickly looked away as if they hadn't been staring at her ass.

"I got the wheels rolling on that thing. Talked to a guy yesterday while I was at the dock. We should be good on that end. Do you have Rick working on something? I mean, I'm assuming you're compartmentalizing the plan so neither of us know the entire thing."

"Good. Good." Grace leaned against the console, facing the opposite direction as Alberto. She wondered if Alberto knew more than he was saying. If he really thought she was giving things to him and Rick piecemeal, or if he had a feeling that she was changing as things moved along. That the plan was fluid, just like the ocean they were rocking on.

"Grace?"

"Rick might be a problem. He's way too focused on my father stealing away his girl. I need to decide what to do with him. I can't have someone distracted like that."

"Grace?"

"What?"

"There's a boat approaching. Starboard. Pretty fast."

Grace turned her head and watched the boat come closer. The two guards noticed it also, one of them speaking to Cuba through his headset.

Cuba was up and out of the water faster than JoJo and Rick. He ripped off his mask and dropped his tank.

"Who is this?" He asked Alberto.

"Why would you think I would know? Probably some drunk college kids who don't know how the hell to drive their daddy's boat." Alberto looked at Grace. "No offense."

Grace shrugged. He was probably right. But something was strange the way it seemed to be heading directly for them when there was so much empty ocean around. It wasn't like they were anchored in the middle of Spring Break.

She recognized the shape before anybody else. There was no mistaking the outline of Ernie Patek holding a drink.

Grace glanced at Cuba and saw recognition in his face a moment later.

The two guards lifted their guns and aimed.

THIRTY-ONE

Baker was alone for the first time in at least a week. While he was enjoying the freedom, he felt lost. Ernie was off doing something and Baker hadn't bothered to ask what Ernie and Maria had planned.

His job was simple: figure out who else was in town and looking for the treasure and/or them.

As if I know how to do that so easily, Baker thought.

He was a paper-shuffler, a pencil-pusher. While saying he was DEA might hold some weight, he'd rarely been in the field working cases. When he was he was usually out there because they were short-staffed and needed bodies.

Baker was the guy that did the coffee runs or formatted reports, while everyone else got to shoot at bad guys and feel like macho men at the end of the day.

He wanted to call his wife but knew it would be a mistake.

By now, protocol for a missing agent meant they'd be searching for him. Maybe not physically at first, but watching his credit cards. Flights. Car rentals. Anything telling them where he was or where he'd been.

Baker knew he'd used his credit card at least a couple of times. The DEA office would know he was in Mexico. They'd wonder why he was in Mexico.

They've likely already talked to my wife, already bugged the phone and are watching from a distance, Baker thought.

She was going to be worried sick. Baker knew this might even affect her health. His biggest fear was she would get sicker without him there and maybe even worse...

He couldn't even think about it.

My wife will be fine. There's nothing to worry about, he thought.

The smart move would be to leave Mexico. Get on the next flight and simply go home. It would give him a few hours to make up a lie about why he was in Mexico and what he'd been doing. The DEA might slap him on the wrist but he was almost positive they weren't going to fire him. He was needed, right? Baker hoped that was the case.

Of course, they could easily get rid of him and hire two college graduates with accounting degrees to do his job and still save money.

Baker felt trapped. By Ernie Patek, by Maria and the cartel, by Cuba, by everyone currently in Mexico also looking for the sunken treasure. More importantly, he felt trapped by his own stupid actions.

The idea of coming to Mexico was to wait for Patek to find the treasure and then step in as a DEA agent and take it from him, never to be seen again.

Not joining forces with the man and now working with him, not only to find the treasure but to stay alive.

Baker had never been this close to the action, the real action, and he knew he wasn't made for this. Sure, he'd been in the field on jobs before, but he had an entire infrastructure to rely on. He had backup and the DEA hovering over his shoulders, ready to swoop in and right everything if he screwed up.

Now, if he screwed up, he might be killed.

There was a good chance of it, too. An even better chance no one would ever find his body, no one would ever know what happened to him. His wife would live the rest of her life with unanswered questions. Baker worried the DEA would sweep it under the rug and never pursue it, either.

Baker Cioffi would simply cease to exist. An agent who died in the line of duty, whatever that duty had actually been.

In reality, the DEA would know he'd gone rogue.

Baker sighed. There might even be agents down in Mexico right now looking for him. How would that work? Would they be here to take him back to the United States? Here to question his motives?

Would they want to kill me since I might be a liability? It's possible, Baker thought.

He wondered who he could trust right now. There weren't many options and none of them were good.

My life has come down to trusting Ernie Patek. I am screwed, Baker thought.

He went down to the corner cafe and ordered a very strong and very small coffee.

No one seemed to be looking at him, no one cared he was in their midst. The town moved to its own beat and one lone gringo wasn't going to change a thing.

Baker's biggest worry was trying to figure out a way to talk to his wife.

He supposed he should be gathering intel right now, but didn't know what that might entail. He didn't even know where to begin.

I'll finish my coffee and go back to the hotel across the street and take a nap. Maybe by then Ernie and Maria will be back, and they've done something important and I don't have to admit I did nothing, Baker thought.

He took the last sip after a few minutes of trying to gather the multitude of thoughts in his head and started to stand when he saw the three black SUVs pull up outside.

This is it. I'm a dead man, Baker thought. He sat back down.

Several men exited the vehicles, their eyes wandering over everyone on the street.

Baker hoped he was far enough away from the entrance to stay hidden. He glanced over his shoulder for an exit but worried if he got up and started to walk toward the back of the cafe he'd be spotted.

All he could do was watch and pray.

The middle SUV's back door opened and a familiar-looking man stepped out into the street, looking around.

Surrounded by cartel thugs, Baker thought.

The men all went inside the hotel, where he was staying.

Baker knew they'd found him and Ernie. Maybe they were with Maria, but he couldn't be sure. Had they gotten lucky, and she'd brought in backup for them?

He doubted it. Not the way it was going for him lately.

Baker watched as the three SUVs pulled away after they'd dropped off the occupants.

It hit him full force when he realized who the man he'd seen that looked familiar was.

DEA Agent George See. A legendary agent with a reputation for getting things done. A man who Baker had had to work with on occasion, and the man was the alpha male in any room.

George made you feel small. He let you know he was going to solve any case and you were there to watch his brilliance.

Baker knew why George See was in town.

He's coming for me. He's on my trail and he knows I'm staying at the hotel. I'm a dead man, Baker thought.

DEA Agent George See was here to eliminate Baker Cioffi, not have a chat with him and accompany him back to the DEA offices for a further talk.

THIRTY-TWO

Maria never had, never would, and never will trust Ernie Patek, but for some reason she was standing on this boat with him, heading toward another boat with his ex-enforcer and who knew how many guns.

Ernie, somehow, had convinced her that he would be able to talk with Cuba without anybody resorting to violence. That he'd known the man well enough and long enough to at least have a temporary ceasefire between them to try to hash things out. Like he was the fucking United Nations or something.

Now, with weapons pointed their way, Maria wasn't so sure. Looking at Ernie, it appeared that his confidence was wavering, also.

After missing her shot at Cuba, Maria had moved them out of her sister's place. They'd spent all of a couple hours there as opposed to the few days she was expecting. Not that her sister was all that upset about it. Maria was barely welcome there. Bringing two men with her – two men who apparently almost ate her entire house – was beyond unacceptable.

But her sister, for as much as she spoke back to her, still knew what Maria was capable of and what she'd done in her past.

Family was family, but to her there was a breaking point for that also.

She'd moved them into a shit hotel, one where she knew the owner and knew he would keep his mouth shut that she was back. Greasing his palms helped reinforce that.

Ernie was upset the place didn't have room service, and complained non-stop until Maria threatened to feed him his nuts.

Baker was quiet. He seemed to be inside his head, thinking about who knew what. Maria assumed it had something to do with his current position and what effect that would have with his job at the agency.

She seemed to remember hearing that his wife was also sick. Baker and Ernie had been talking about it on the boat after they'd somehow gotten the drop on her and Raul and tied them up below deck.

Baker was probably the only one out of all of them trying to get a piece of the treasure for a decent moral reason, and not just selfishness. Maria would probably feel bad for him if she allowed herself to feel anything at all.

She was too busy berating herself for missing Cuba and hitting the kid, Arturo.

Even though she knew it wasn't her fault, it still didn't make her feel any better. Despite her ruthless reputation in the cartel, Maria had a thing about hurting children. Probably because she had one of her own. If the cartel knew, it would be seen as a weakness. Her being a female and in charge was a position she was challenged on constantly anyway. Having a child meant having a crack in her facade that other people could use to exploit her, and thereby exploit the cartel.

Ernie had brought up confronting Cuba while Baker was in the bathroom. She had no illusions that Baker couldn't hear what was being said. You could hear a sneeze through the hotel walls.

Ernie was a moron, though, and spoke without even trying to lower his voice.

His idea was to find Cuba, call a truce, and then work something out where they all win when the treasure was found. He also wanted to make sure Grace was alright and, if possible, get her out of that situation.

Maria asked him if he knew where the actual treasure was. So far he'd provided a fake map, a false claim that the real location was burned into his memory, and fake GPS coordinates on a boat that was now a shipwreck of its own.

For the first time, Ernie had been honest with her and told her he had, in his own words, 'no fucking idea' where the treasure was. He claimed that he knew there was one, and that all the false leads had been on purpose to throw off anyone trying to steal it from him. But the problem was he had never been able to find anyone who knew exactly where it was. He knew the general area, but that covered miles of water and would take a lifetime to dive.

Maria agreed, stupidly, she thought as they continued to get closer to the boat. They had told Baker to wait at the hotel and he seemed fine with it. Too fine. She assumed he was more than happy to have nothing to do with Cuba and his men. She wouldn't be surprised if he was gone, headed back to the U.S., when they got back. If they made it back.

Maria kept waiting to hear gunshots. She'd braced her legs to either drop to the floor of the boat, or dive overboard. Considering that Cuba had blown up the previous boat that had gotten in his way of the treasure, right in front of witnesses, she wouldn't put anything past him.

"Tell me again that this is going to be okay," Maria said.

"It's going to be okay."

"You don't sound as convinced as you were in the hotel."

"That would be because I'm not." Ernie took a sip from the tequila he'd taken from below deck after transferring a large amount of money to the boat's owner in order to take it out by themselves for the day.

Maria absentmindedly touched the handle of the gun tucked into the back of her pants. If the situation turned into a shoot out, at least she'd be able to take off the back of Cuba's head. It would dampen all the plans she'd had for the treasure, since she'd almost definitely be killed as well, but at least she'd take that bastard with her.

No shots sounded out, and as the boat slowed, Ernie turned it so it was lengthwise with Cuba's boat. Once it drifted in five feet from the other boat, he pressed the button to drop anchor and turned to face the man who had not only betrayed him in business, but in his personal life as well.

Maria saw a beautiful young woman standing by Cuba and assumed that was Grace. Even if she didn't know the story behind the girl's birth, she would know right away that the kid wasn't Ernie's.

"I don't know if you got some kind of brain damage since I last saw you, but I'm giving you one warning to get the hell out of here before I sink both of you and the boat," Cuba said.

"Give me one minute of your time and then I'll be out of your hair," Ernie said.

"How did you find us?"

"Trade secret. You want to chat or do you want to hear what I have to say?"

"Neither, really. But I'll give you your minute." Cuba looked at his dive watch. Maria was pretty sure he literally meant one minute.

"I have a pretty simple proposal. Grace for the mafia chick."

"What?" Maria asked. The statement had come as too much of a shock for her to react.

Ernie pulled the gun from her waistband and pressed it against her head.

"I don't give a shit about the treasure anymore, Cuba. I'm fucking exhausted. All this moving around. The damn heat. Nobody ever has enough food. I want to get back to California where normal people live. And I want to do it with my daughter."

"You mean my daughter?"

"Semantics. You never gave a shit about her. You're just holding onto her because you know it gives you leverage over me. But now you can have Maria. You know what that gives you? Leverage over the cartel. And that's much more lucrative than anything you can get out of me. So how about it?"

Maria twisted, trying to take Ernie by surprise and get her gun back, but he dodged and clipped her on the back of the head. She dropped to the boat floor, her vision spinning and her hearing muted.

She didn't hear the rest of the conversation, but next thing she knew she was being lifted up and tossed over to the other boat. She landed hard on the floor and before passing out heard a single gunshot.

THIRTY-THREE

George See was never in over his head. He always knew the players, always knew the best way to get what he wanted and always knew the exits. Even in a town like this, in Mexico, where everyone had a price.

That price, he was realizing, wasn't too big, either.

He'd taken care of Nigel and Mike, knowing there was no going back for him. He was either going to start a new life as a key member of the cartel or die trying.

The ultimate rush, George thought. Not trying to shut down the players but being the player. Alpha male. The big fish in a small pond.

It wasn't like this was anything new for him, either. He'd been on the payroll of The Wolf for the last four years. Made sure to feed him information from both the DEA and the FBI whenever possible. George had made sure nothing major ever happened to the cartels.

Yes, cartels. Plural. He smiled as he thought of the money coming in from working with several, big and small. Of course, none of them knew he worked for anyone but them. He'd hand out information as he deemed appropriate, so no one cartel could gain absolute power.

Why consolidate your payday into one when you could have a dozen, all paying you the same amount? At this rate George See would be able to retire in three years.

He'd step away from the DEA. He hadn't worked out the proper way to do it just yet, but he had a plan in place. Maybe a gunshot wound, nowhere that would do any real damage. Go out a hero.

Maybe he'd act like he'd burned out. That was a common way an agent stepped aside and retired, although it didn't seem flashy enough for George.

He craved the excitement, the huge exit.

Jerry Maguire way of doing things, George thought. The big burst of energy, the things he'd always wanted to say, flailing his arms and shouting.

George knew that might sound cool but it'd be the wrong way to do it. The perfect way was to hand in his resignation, say he was done and thank the DEA for the opportunity. He needed to take some time off and not look back.

That was the way to retire without drawing any attention, because once he stepped away he knew it wouldn't just be from the DEA but from the cartels, too.

The DEA might hand him a gold watch for his service and a decent severance, but the cartels would put a price on his head for no longer working for them.

Information was never going to run out, and George knew he'd need to put into motion a new life and soon. New identity, a new look, a safe place to go off the grid and hide.

Right now, he was in his hotel room staring out the window at the peasants on the street below. He'd asked the cartel to put him up in a decent hotel but not the fanciest.

The fear was Ernie Patek and Baker Cioffi would be in the five-star hotel, if one even existed in this armpit of the world, and George didn't want to be seen.

This was a stealth mission. Off the books. He knew his bosses were going to send agents down to Mexico to check in on the movements of Patek and they wondered where Cioffi had gone off to.

George had taken some vacation time and figured out which agents were on their way to Mexico and cut them off before they had time to learn anything.

If I was smart, I would've let them do the heavy lifting and found Patek or Cioffi, George thought.

He couldn't chance them finding more than he was comfortable with them finding. What if Patek had finally found something worthwhile? The fat man had a lot of plans and a lot of irons in the fire, but to George they never seemed to work out.

If this was finally Patek's time, George wanted to be the only one who was there at the end of the rainbow to collect the pot of gold.

He was in constant contact with three cartel groups right now that were active in the area, but knew the Sinaloa Cartel was the big dog. They were the one he needed to appease and continue to help while he was in town.

It was risky because if he did anything one of their drug-addled bosses thought was suspect, he could be taken out. He presented a nice target as a DEA agent, too.

George See didn't want to die a hero or a martyr. He wanted to die an old man on a beach, richer than anyone he knew, quietly passing during a nice nap.

He started to count out the tens and fives he'd brought into Mexico, smiling at how easy it was to pay people off. At how easy these Mexicans were when it came to a bribe. When it comes to information.

George had already contacted the mayor and the chief of police, who would be there shortly. Even though they both already worked for the cartel, he wanted to personally meet with both of them to show how serious he was about what he was doing and who he was looking for.

He'd shake their hands with fifty dollars in tens to start the process. Grease the political wheels.

With a hundred U.S. dollars he could have the two most powerful men in town working for him.

Not as powerful as I am, not as powerful as the cartel is, but still at the top of the civilian pile, George thought.

George also knew he couldn't freely roam. Not that he'd want to. He needed to stay hidden and conduct his work from this window seat, because of fear of being seen by the wrong people.

If other cartels knew where he was they'd get worried he was doing something against them. He was supposed to let them know if he was going to be in Mexico or anywhere south of this point.

By showing up unannounced, George was putting himself in jeopardy.

He knew there were other players in town he needed to be worried about, but right now he couldn't be bothered. Patek and Cioffi were his only focus.

The goal would be to capture both and torture them until they spilled the reason they were here. Then he'd kill them both, take whatever it is they were looking for or had acquired, and fly back to his home.

In The United States, away from these third-world idiots and the dust and the dirt and the smells. If he was lucky, not only would he get to kill again but he'd be able to add to his coffers and maybe retire six months earlier than planned.

Depending on what Patek and Cioffi were looking for or had found.

He knew this wasn't a pleasure trip for them. In order for Cioffi to have seemingly thrown his career out the window, this meant big money was involved.

George See was going to figure it out, because he was the best at what he did.

THIRTY-FOUR

This is all bullshit, Rick thought, watching the exchange between Cuba and Patek.

He'd just recently made a deal with Maria to get her information to take Cuba down, and now she was being handed over as a captive for him to do whatever he wanted to her.

Rick needed her alive and free, and by the look on Cuba's face when she was tossed onto the boat, his plan was most likely to torture and kill her.

He was stewing in thought that he missed some of the conversation, and only came out of his own head when he heard yelling.

Grace was screaming at Cuba who was having his men attempt to hand her over to Ernie. By the looks of it, she'd gotten one really good in the shin and balls. The other guard still had her in a bear hug, but seemed really protective of his own junk.

"What the hell is your problem? You never wanted to be here anyway. And besides, a deal is a deal," Cuba said.

"I'm not a part of any deal. I'm a person. You can't just trade me around. I'm not going with him. I'm staying right here."

"Grace, what's wrong with you?" Ernie asked. "Just come over and we can be done with this. Back to California and only having to deal with socialist morons instead of crazy people with guns."

Rick tried to think if there was anything he could do while they were distracted and one of the guards was incapacitated on the ground holding his nuts. But what would that be? He didn't have a gun, and if he did he wouldn't be able to take out Cuba, Ernie, and the two guards. He'd be dead after one shot. Even leaving Ernie out of the equation, he wouldn't make it.

Maria was on the ground looking dazed and about to pass out.

JoJo was off to the side, watching the yelling match, still dripping in her wetsuit. If Rick had a chance of getting her back, this may be the only opening he had to begin that process. Otherwise, whether she liked it or not, Grace would be handed over and Cuba would have his attention divided.

The more he thought about the situation he'd allowed them to get stuck in, the more Rick began fuming.

This was supposed to be simple. JoJo butters up Patek, gets the treasure map, and they go out and get it. Simple. She wasn't even supposed to steal the map off him. The original plan had been to wait until he fell asleep and just take pictures of it. That way Ernie would never know, and the treasure would be long gone before he had even begun to put his crew together to dive.

Somehow that simple plan had turned into the giant mess he was currently watching. The entire thing made Rick think about his old friend Johnny and his big ideas that always turned to shit. Maybe he'd spent too much time around incompetent friends that their ways had rubbed off on him.

Rick checked the tank gauge, spit into his mask and rubbed it around. Behind him, JoJo and Alberto watched the scene, both not moving. He gave JoJo a look, knowing after all the years together she would understand what it meant.

JoJo's mouth tightened and she shook her head.

Rick backed up until he hit the dash of the boat. He remembered there was a first aid cabinet on that side of the boat. Alberto had gotten some items from there a few times when someone had a minor injury during a dive, or just misadventures on the boat.

He also remembered seeing something else in there. Something Cuba and his guards, all obviously not too aware of what was and wasn't stored on most boats, had overlooked when first securing the vessel to make sure none of them got the drop.

Rick opened the first aid drawer and rooted around blindly with his hand, switching his gaze between Cuba and Ernie to make sure neither saw what he was doing.

His hand grabbed onto the flare gun and he pulled it from the clamps that were holding it in place. Rick adjusted it so he was ready to point and waited for the right moment.

As stupid and selfish as it probably was, he wanted Cuba looking at him when he shot the bastard.

The moment presented itself a few seconds later when Cuba, exasperated by Grace's fighting, turned to address her directly. Rick, just off to the right of her, pulled out the flare gun and aimed it at him.

Cuba's eyes shifted immediately to Rick. He didn't look as surprised as Rick had hoped he would. In fact, he looked just annoyed at yet another complication.

Rick had seen plenty of movies where the bad guy was taken out by a flare gun. It seemed realistic and he never doubted that when he pulled the trigger, Cuba would be gut punched with the round and burst into flames. Hopefully he'd flail around a bit on the boat, burning up, and then jump into the ocean and die.

Turns out killing someone with a flare gun was just more Hollywood bullshit.

Rick pulled the trigger, the shot sounding more like a pop than the loud gunshot he was expecting. The flare hit Cuba in the chest, who grunted but didn't flinch, bounced off him, and careened into the water.

Rick watched the glow from the flare fade out as it sank.

Nobody moved. Even Grace stopped yelling and looked at him. Rick felt like he'd farted in church or something.

"Really?" Cuba asked. "Did you think that was a smart move, or were you just not thinking at all?"

"Can't kill someone with a flare, dude," Grace said.

Rick's plan had been to shoot Cuba and then dive out, get to the shore, and find help. Pretend that he and JoJo were just innocent expats who were kidnapped by this maniac because they happened to be skilled divers. Anything that would focus the authorities on Cuba and not them long enough to pack up and disappear to another town, or another country.

He debated jumping overboard anyway, but he couldn't swim faster than a bullet. And Cuba definitely wouldn't care if he was out of the way. Now that he thought about it, Rick was surprised Cuba hadn't found some way for him to run into an accident. It must have meant that he was keeping him around for a reason.

Did that mean he'd make it through this fuck up, also? Or was Rick breathing his last few breaths?

"Give me your gun," Cuba told the guard.

"Wait," JoJo said.

Rick pushed her back, away from him and the path of what was coming his way.

Cuba racked a round in the chamber, looked at Rick, then turned and fired the entire clip into the side of Ernie's boat.

Ernie dove to the ground, cursing.

"Let's go. Let the fat man sink. Grace wants to stay, she can stay."

Cuba handed the gun back to his guard before giving Rick one more look and heading below.

Alberto started the boat and took off, leaving Ernie and his cursing behind them as they drove around the bend and out of sight.

THIRTY-FIVE

Ignacio was panicking. It was low tide right now, and the treasure chest was clearly visible. He looked up and down the beach, glad no one ever came out here but him.

But all it would take was a nosy tourist or a couple looking to fool around and it would be found.

He imagined if it happened and there was a big deal made of it. A newspaper article, front page, with some idiot smiling with a hand on the top of the opened lid and the chest overflowing with gold.

Maybe I can figure out a way to open it and try to take small amounts home and hide it, Ignacio thought.

Based on how big the chest was and assuming it would be filled to the top, that might take weeks or maybe even a couple of months if he simply filled his pockets, unless he made dozens of trips a day. Then someone would notice him and eventually figure out what was happening.

No, he needed to get someone else involved.

Ignacio knew it wasn't his crew, either. They were just kids. If they saw even one gold coin they'd talk about it. Tell a parent or other kids. Within a couple of days it would all be gone, scattered across town.

He waded out to the chest, hoping he could simply open it and see inside. He'd tried it before but maybe it was just stuck and not locked.

Ignacio knew he was fooling himself if he thought he could pry it open. Even if he had a crowbar he doubted he was going to be strong enough to break the lock or pop the top.

As he got nearer he saw sailboats in the distance and hoped none of them sailed closer to shore. Not that he thought they'd be able to see the chest, but if they used binoculars they had a small chance.

Even a small chance of losing the treasure was too much for Ignacio to think about.

Ignacio stood next to the chest and smiled.

There was another chest directly underneath the exposed one, and when he scraped away some sand he saw there was at least a third down there, too.

A bigger treasure than even I knew, he thought.

There was no way he could move this himself, especially now. Heck, there might be a dozen chests sunken underneath where he stood.

I need to figure out a way to sink this one so when the tide rolls out no one can see it, Ignacio thought.

He tried to shake the chest back and forth but it was no use. Whatever was inside – and he knew without a doubt it was gold and silver coins, fabulous jewelry and precious gems – was too heavy to move at all.

Ignacio needed to cover it, but that might bring more attention to it. There were no natural formations this close to the beach, no reefs or large rocks in the ocean.

He decided he'd need to come back with a crowbar or an ax and chop into the side of it, with the hope he could spill the contents into the water and break up the chest so it was no longer exposed.

But how? A boy walking through town with an ax over his shoulder would draw too much attention. Even in this town.

He knew he needed to tell Maria or Rick, but didn't know which one made more sense. If either of them did.

His worst fears kept coming back to him: either of them would simply take it, or they'd involve bad people who would take it. Maybe by pulling one of them in Ignacio would be putting everyone in danger.

There had to be a way to do this, but right now he was at a loss.

Instead of hanging around and maybe being seen, Ignacio walked back to the beach and headed for home. No use in dwelling on it. There was an answer but it wouldn't be simple.

The goal now was to gather fake intel for Cuba and hope it was enough to keep the man handing out money, so his crew would get some and stay focused and busy.

I do this all for my mother, whichever one is really my mother, and for my future. I don't want to be a street urchin my entire life, and moving up and into the cartel ranks as a soldier is not appealing, Ignacio thought.

This should be a way out of this town and perhaps even Mexico. He watched enough American television shows to know it was better to the north, across the border. The land of the free and the home of the brave.

Streets lined with gold and all the soda and potato chips you would ever need. Everyone drove fancy cars and took three and four showers each day, and rode horses. Ignacio wanted to wear a cowboy hat and eventually become what he'd heard called a True Southerner.

He'd be a man of the people, his new people, and he'd be wealthy and happy and rich.

The treasure could open any door for him and his family, and lead to great things.

If it didn't get them all killed first.

Rick or Maria?

Ignacio shook his head when he got inside his home. His mother was in the kitchen and he didn't feel like talking to her, so he slipped into his room and quietly closed the door.

The other people had all left, which was fine with him.

Ignacio dropped down onto his bed and closed his eyes. He was going to think long and hard about a solution to his current problem.

In a couple of hours he'd gather his crew and they'd figure out if anyone had learned anything. He hoped they had a couple of clues, some tidbits, but nothing substantial.

When working with a client, especially a new one, you need to be careful how much information you give to them in the beginning. Enough to make it seem like you knew what you were doing but not enough for them to figure they had what they needed and would move on to their own devices.

Ignacio would need to play this just right, because Cuba might be a lot to handle. From what he'd heard from Rick and Maria, this man was the real deal.

He would be relentless in his pursuit of the treasure.

One slip of the tongue and Ignacio could end up in the ocean, dead and bloated, next to the treasure chests.

He smiled. There was more than one of them, which meant even more treasure to spend the rest of his long lifetime.

Ignacio just needed a solid plan to extract the treasure without anyone knowing, without prying eyes seeing what he was doing.

They'd know, in the end, because he'd be wealthy and gone.

Ignacio decided he would spread a little of it in town because they were still his people, it was still his birthplace, but no one would ever know it was from him.

No one would ever know where he and his mother had run off to, either.

THIRTY-SIX

Baker grabbed the few things he had and left the hotel room. He didn't give a damn about any of Ernie or Maria's items. He just wanted to get out of the room and hopefully out of the hotel and far away before Agent See found him.

From the looks of the group of people who he'd arrived with, this wasn't a sanctioned assignment from the DEA. Baker knew cartel men when he saw them.

Since they knew he was here, he assumed they also knew what room he was staying in. He was surprised that George had allowed them to pull up to the front like that. He'd have been better off parking a couple blocks away and then walking in a back door. Baker would have had no idea they were even here until it was too late.

It could be Agent See was getting over-confident. He'd always been a pompous asshole, but what made him dangerous was that he could actually back up his feelings of superiority over any of the other agents.

The only hope Baker had of staying alive was to get out of the building without being seen. Otherwise, he'd be in the hands of See and the cartel, and he wasn't sure which one was worse.

He opened the door a crack and looked into the hallway. Nobody was loitering out on that side. He opened it further and peered around the edge. Nobody over there, either.

Baker left the room, bypassing the elevator and heading to the end of the hallway where the stairs were. It was possible Agent See would send men up the stairs, but it was absolutely certain that there would be men waiting in the lobby.

He'd rather play hide and seek in the stairwell than walk out of the elevator and immediately get surrounded.

He stepped into the stairwell and listened. No footsteps from above or below, but that didn't mean there weren't people coming. These weren't sloppy mercenaries Agent See was with.

Baker tried to remember his training. Too many years at a desk had basically turned him back into a civilian. The stealth and counter-measure tactics drilled into them as recruits tended to fade away if they weren't used.

He also really wished he'd looked for a weapon in the room instead of panicking and rushing out.

He made his way down. There were only a few flights to get through, so if he was going to run into anybody it would happen soon.

Baker winced at the sound of his feet bouncing off the walls. He could have been more careful, but he was still in panic mode and wanted out as quickly as possible. As he rounded the corner to the next flight, he saw the heads of two men coming up.

Baker tried the door next to him that led to the third floor hallway, but it was locked. He never understood why hotels had to lock doors to certain floors, and now he still didn't understand and was also pissed off on top of it.

A fire hose in a glass case was on one wall. He looked at it carefully, checking to see if an alarm would go off when the door to the case was opened.

Seeing no signs and no sensors, Baker held his breath and pulled the handle. Other than the two men coming up the stairs, the stairwell remained quiet.

He grabbed hold of the end and wrapped a length around his arm, slipping the loop off his elbow. This wasn't from training. He thought he might have seen this in one of those Bourne movies.

The two men rounded the corner. Baker hesitated, not wanting to take down a couple of innocent hotel guests. The guns in each of their hands gave them away.

He rounded the corner and flung the coiled hose at them. The metal end hit one of the men in the head, making a sickening crunch sound and he had enough time to see him collapse before moving out of sight as the other man fired his weapon.

Footsteps ran up toward him and Baker, having no other option, flung himself at the guy as he hit the top step. The two of them toppled down to the next landing. He was pinned under the man and getting elbowed in the side as he held onto his arm, keeping the guy from using his gun.

Through sheer luck, he found leverage to flip over and gain the advantage. He grabbed the fire hose and wrapped it a couple times around the man's neck before pulling as hard as he could.

It took way too long for the body to become still.

Baker backed off, breathing heavily. Because of the gunshots, he only had a limited time to get the hell out of the hotel, but he needed a minute to slow his breathing. Making it out of the building wouldn't help if he dropped from a heart attack in the alley.

He made it to the bottom without another incident and pushed through the door and outside. He should have checked the alley first, but it was too late. Luckily, nobody was stationed there waiting for him.

Baker didn't know what to do from here. He needed to get away, but had no idea how he was going to make it anywhere safe. He had no transportation, and the only person he'd met who would help him was not only a criminal, but was also currently out with yet another cartel member trying to find a homicidal maniac to negotiate splitting treasure.

He looked down the end of the alley leading away from the hotel, but it ended at a cinder block wall with razor wire on the top. There were only two options: sneak out toward the front of the building and hope he wasn't seen, or go back into the hotel, which didn't make any sense.

Baker headed to the road in front of him. When he got to the end of the alley he peeked around the corner.

The cars were still parked out front. Not surprising, since they obviously hadn't found him yet. A couple men waited with the vehicles, strapped with automatic weapons. They didn't appear to be too observant, talking with each other and occasionally looking around.

He wondered if they even knew what he looked like. Agent See probably thought he had the drop on him and this would turn out to be an easy catch. No need to brief every single person on the team with all the details.

But Baker would rather be cautious than be caught.

He waited until the two men turned their backs, then began to step out and stopped in his tracks.

Ernie Patek was coming up the street toward the hotel, seemingly oblivious to the SUVs outside and the armed men. He was also soaking wet and looked a little more than pissed off.

Baker stood out as much as he dared, trying to wave an arm and warn Ernie not to go inside. It was useless. Whatever plan he and Maria had (and where was Maria?) had obviously gone wrong. And when Ernie was pissed off, he didn't pay attention to anything but his emotions.

Ernie went through the hotel doors and less than a minute later he was dragged out, screaming, with Agent See following behind.

They threw Patek into one of the vehicles, and the entire team loaded in. Baker put his back against the wall and watched the cars speed past him. He thought he caught a glimpse of Ernie in the backseat, still screaming and fighting.

Then, it was silent again.

Baker adjusted his pack with all the belongings he had left in the world, chose a direction, and began walking.

THIRTY-SEVEN

Maria kept her smile on her face, despite the danger she was currently in. No way was she going to show Cuba any fear, even if she thought her life was going to end soon enough.

She watched with the rest of them as Ernie's boat was slowly sinking, thinking the fat man was going to be unable to swim back to shore. Not as big as he was, although maybe he could simply float and enjoy himself.

"This is bullshit," Grace said. She was looking at the sinking boat and her father. "You should've taken him with us or shot him, Cuba. That seems cruel, even for you."

"He'll survive. Ernie Patek is like a cockroach. A really fat, bloated cockroach. In the end, despite everything we do or don't do, I will bet you he'll still be there." Cuba shook his head and laughed, turning to Maria. "What about you?"

"What about me? I'm not a cockroach."

Cuba shrugged. "The way I'm describing Ernie, it isn't a bad thing. I'm wondering what the two of you have been scheming, and where you left Baker."

"Ernie had the dumb sense to bargain with you. Have us all join together for the common goal of finding the treasure, figuring there would be more than enough to split it and we'd all live happily ever after," Maria said.

"And you disagreed?" Grace asked.

Maria smiled. "I knew you weren't smart enough to listen to reason. I also knew your ego would get in the way, because men like you are always driven by ego and your dick. Right, Cuba?"

"You do have a point," Cuba said with a chuckle. "But those two things, my ego and my dick, have gotten me this far. Why change anything now, right? I guess you'll come with us. For now."

Maria turned to JoJo and Grace. "You're all following him around blindly now? Alliances keep changing like the wind. Who else is on your team?"

"Rick," JoJo said.

Maria smiled again. "And where is Rick?"

"Down below. He, uh…" Grace shrugged. "He tried to kill Cuba with a flare gun. Shot him in the chest."

"That doesn't do anything. Maybe if you get lucky it will set clothes on fire and leave a mark," Maria said.

"Yeah, Rick found that out after the fact. He probably won't do that again," Grace said.

Maria wanted to keep the dialogue going for a couple of reasons: to see what they knew and if they were close to finding the treasure, and to figure out where she fit in.

The worst-case scenario would be Cuba, who was obviously leading the group, didn't think Maria would help him to find the treasure. If she was dead weight, she'd be dead sooner than later.

"Ernie didn't know anything anyway," Maria said. "This was all a bluff from him."

"I'm starting to realize that. And yet... there is a treasure. I'm sure of it. Back when all of this started, Ernie did have a real map. Not the one he'd forged to sell to the cartel." Cuba shook his head. "While he was definitely interested in whatever was down there, it was more exciting to show his supposed superiority. Ernie wanted to mess with the cartel and send them off one way while he eventually found the treasure."

"But why piss off the cartel? It makes no sense," Maria said.

"Because that's who my father is. I remember when I was a teenager and we went on a skiing trip to Finland or Sweden, supposedly just for fun," Grace said. "But he was really there to steal some precious gems from a church. Not on his own, of course. Ernie was the distraction while a group of others got in and switched the gems with fakes my father had made. No one ever knew about the switch. As far as I know, he never saw the thieves again and had no interest in collecting any of his money he'd spent back. Why? Because it wasn't the kill, it was the thrill of the chase. That's what he always said."

"I don't care who ends up with the treasure as long as I'm cut into the deal. Simple as that," Maria said.

"Then help us and we'll be fair to you." JoJo said it to Maria but she was staring at Cuba.

"What? Fine. She can help us to find it and then she can get a fair share. There will be more than enough for all of us." Cuba sat down and stared into the distance.

Alberto was silently piloting the boat, and Maria knew that man had some thoughts running through his head. He was an observer, but he was listening to every conversation. She was sure Alberto was also being promised a fair share, but like everyone else, it was a crapshoot whether he'd survive to the end.

Rick came up from below and nodded at Maria, as if it was nothing new. As if they were going to keep popping in and out of each other's lives until they found the treasure.

And then it would likely be the last man or woman standing, Maria thought.

"I heard you tried to kill Cuba with a flare gun, like in a movie," Maria said to Rick and grinned. "Where did you see that?'

Rick shrugged. "I think in a Jason Bourne one. Not sure. I thought it would hit him hard enough he'd fall backwards into the water and then I could either take control of the boat and leave him, or it would rip through his body, his heart exploding, and we'd be done with him."

Cuba chuckled. "Have I been that bad to you so far, Rick? I thought we were getting along nicely."

Maria saw the dark look on Rick's face and knew this was more than annoyance. Rick hated Cuba, and she thought she might be able to use it to her advantage in the future.

Maybe Cuba and JoJo are an item now. A man who's lost his girl to another man is dangerous. Also reckless, which isn't good, Maria thought.

"Where are we headed?" Maria asked Cuba.

"Back to the villa. We'd done a couple of dives already today but nothing came of it. I know it is here... but where?" Cuba shrugged and stared out again.

"Ernie is going to be so pissed," Grace said.

Maria knew the fat man would somehow survive. What Cuba had said about him was true. The easiest thing to think about Ernie was that he'd drown and they'd be done with him.

It wasn't too far to shore, and he might already be pulling himself onto a beach, soaking wet and angry.

"I will join you and hope we can find the treasure," Maria said. "I have men at my disposal."

Men who will do my bidding and not Cuba's bidding, and will kill every one of you if I give the order, Maria thought.

She needed to remain calm, learn all she could and then take Cuba and the other's out... once they'd helped her to locate the treasure, of course.

Maria never wanted to waste her time killing people if it couldn't do her good in the long run.

She turned her head up to the sun and closed her eyes with a smile.

THIRTY-EIGHT

They hadn't covered his head with a pillowcase or something else. That wasn't a good sign. Ernie had been through enough kidnappings in his life to know that you had a better chance of being let go when your vision was covered.

Apparently, they didn't seem to care if he knew where they were taking him, or seeing their faces. Not a good situation to be in.

Ernie Patek never had any grandiose feeling about himself. A little ego, sure. But never thought he was something he wasn't. He knew he wasn't the smartest person, certainly not in the best shape, and a little slow on pulling the trigger on anything. What he counted on more than anything else in his life was luck.

Almost every tricky situation he'd found himself in, he had managed to squeak by, barely avoiding any serious harm.

He never knew how he was able to pull it off. Maybe his lack of forethought helped. He never got bogged down with 'what-ifs' and all that nonsense. Every moment in life was the present. The past was gone and the future didn't exist, so there was no point worrying over anything that hadn't happened yet.

Ernie'd gotten that hippie shit from his mom. His father never gave him anything but a couple black eyes and a hell of a lot of mental abuse about his weight.

The SUV bounced on the ruts, knocking Ernie into the men on either side of him. They both shoved him with their elbows, careful to keep him out of reach of their weapons. As if he'd attempt to take them away. He wasn't that dumb.

Ernie didn't smell gunpowder from either of them, so at least they hadn't fired the weapons inside the hotel. For a moment before they all piled on him in the lobby, he was sure they were just going to spray him full of holes.

Then some American macho man type tells them to grab him and put him in the car. Ernie had never seen the guy before, and he obviously had some control in the cartel if the men were taking orders from him. That meant one of two things: the guy was ex-alphabet; DEA, CIA, or any of the others. The cartel loved bringing in rogue agents. Probably something to do with being able to turn the country's highest trained assets to their favor. The other option was that the man was a civilian brought in by the cartel, which was scarier.

Civilians who dealt with the cartel at any level tended to outlast their welcome fast. Over time, Ernie had instinctively learned how to get in and get out with any plans that he needed to involve the cartel in. To have an American citizen with no formal government background training acting as head of a team of cartel men meant the guy was extremely dangerous and just as crazy as the chainsaw wielding, chop-your-legs-off people in the group.

The American was in the front passenger seat, not saying a word. This was obviously a planned attack, but Ernie couldn't think of why they would be after him. Granted, this entire treasure situation was one giant shit show, and he hadn't exactly been the best around the cartel. But Maria had, at least for now, taken his side. The only other person he'd been involved with was Raul, and he was long gone.

Did Maria go behind his back and alert her superiors to grab him? That didn't make sense. She could have just clocked him over the head with her gun at any time. Instead, she went with him to try to make a truce with Cuba, or so Ernie had told her, and gotten herself taken.

Maybe Cuba used her to get to him? Cuba had been his right-hand-man long enough to see the ridiculous situation he'd been able to get out of. To see Ernie's luck in action. He had to know that he would have most likely not drowned. Maybe Cuba had Maria rat him out in exchange for something else. Take him out of the picture and gain an additional advantage.

It still didn't explain the American, remaining silent in the front seat.

What seemed to take forever, was probably only a thirty-minute drive. The caravan stopped at a gate, opened it, and headed down the freshly paved driveway to a large, yet modest house with no neighbors in view.

Men with guns patrolled the grounds. A couple stood on the roof. But other than that, this could be any upper middle class family's Mexican retreat. It didn't shout cartel money. Whoever's place it was either lived modestly or used this house for things he didn't want done on his main property.

Ernie hoped for the former.

The two men with guns and the driver exited the vehicle with a signal from the American. Ernie adjusted himself in the backseat, finally able to have a little elbow room. His clothes had dried, except for the parts touching the seat. He had to pull those away from his body.

"I'm going to ask you this before we go inside. I'd advise you to answer honestly, because once we go in I have no control over what might happen to you. I do know that whatever it is will not be pleasant." The American stared at him. Just his look made Ernie uncomfortable.

"Well, it hasn't exactly been a pleasant day anyway. Take a dive into the ocean. Probably came within feet of getting eaten by sharks. God knows I look like the biggest fucking seal they've ever encountered. Then I get to the hotel and you grab me without a hello or anything. Right around free brunch time, too. But ask your question. I'll decide how I answer once I know what the hell you want from me."

"See, the problem is, I'm going to walk you in there and the man inside will be happy to see you. But he won't be as happy to see me, since I've only accomplished half of my job. The sooner I can remedy that, the better. So, please tell me where Baker Cioffi is."

Now the last piece of the puzzle fell. Whoever he was, he must be a DEA turncoat, still active but rogue, or an ex-agent. Either way, Ernie would have to make sure he remained helpful to him in finding Baker. After that, he'd see what would happen.

"That's easy, he's in the hotel. Guess you jumped the gun when you saw me."

The American shook his head. "No. My men checked your room. Baker wasn't there. It looks like he spotted us, packed his shit, before killing two cartel men and escaping. Certainly took me by surprise, that little desk jockey still has some moves left."

"Well, then I have no idea. And you have to know I'm speaking the truth. I told you the last place I saw him. But I can help you find him. He's not the best in this type of life, but I've gotten to know him pretty well. To know his habits. He'll try to get out of town quietly, maybe by bus. Some public transportation where he thinks he can blend in with the locals."

"Not much help. Let's go see the man."

"No, wait. He doesn't like being uncomfortable, out of control in these situations. He'll do something familiar, go somewhere familiar."

"Where's that?"

"Back to Mexico City. Then probably on the first plane out of the country. Take a look at buses leaving from town and heading that way. Considering you have a rough idea of when he took off, it shouldn't be hard to narrow it down and stop the bus long before it reached the city."

The American nodded. He got out of the car and motioned for Ernie to follow. He never thought he'd just be let go because he'd helped with the Baker situation, but it would bring some goodwill. This was probably all about the treasure, anyway. It's not like he'd killed some cartel boss's family or anything.

"Who are we going to see?"

"Diego Santiago. Ring a bell?"

"No. I'm not all up in cartel business anyway."

"Mr Santiago wants to talk to you about his brother, Raul. Specifically about his murder." The American glanced at Ernie with a smirk.

He was going to need to call on a lot more luck than he thought he would to get out of this alive.

THIRTY-NINE

Rick was staring at JoJo. The two of them had retired to their room after all the excitement. While Rick had wanted to grab something to eat and drink upon arriving, he saw Cuba, Maria, Grace and Alberto were heading toward the kitchen.

He'd lightly touched JoJo's arm and motioned for her to follow him upstairs to the room.

They walked out onto the balcony and huddled close together. You never knew if there were cameras and microphones everywhere.

"I need you to be honest with me," Rick whispered. He had his hand over his mouth so no one watching, if there was anyone watching, could read his lips. "Where are you in all of this?"

"Trying to survive," JoJo said into her own hand. "You?"

"Same, but..." Rick was worried he'd already lost JoJo to Cuba, but he couldn't come right out and ask her about it. Not because he thought she'd lie, but because he thought she'd tell the truth and say she was now with Cuba.

"Are you back on drugs? Heroin or something new this time?" JoJo asked.

"Nothing." Rick shook his head. "I swear."

"You've sworn before you were clean, but it was all a lie. How can I trust you? We're in constant danger and you're throwing it all away for a cheap high. I don't get it." JoJo sighed. "I know what you want to ask, so ask it."

Rick was silent. He didn't want to know the answer, which he already knew in his heart. He'd screwed up and lost JoJo. Even though he hadn't fallen off the wagon and started doing drugs and fallen into old habits, she'd never believe him. What good was he if she couldn't trust him? They'd survived this long together because of trust. When all was said and done, they were a team that needed to rely on the other every step of the way.

And I blew it, Rick thought.

"We've survived worse than this," JoJo said. "And it wasn't too long ago, either. We need to stay focused and keep our eyes open. There is a way out of this for both of us, and a door will open. Something will present itself and we need to take it."

"I suppose." Rick stared off and saw the ripple of the heat on the ocean a few blocks away. He knew sooner than later they'd be back on Alberto's boat and diving again. Over and over.

JoJo kissed Rick on the cheek and went back inside.

Was that a kiss goodbye? Am I overthinking everything as usual? Life was simpler when I was a drug-addled FBI agent getting by, he thought.

He'd done what he swore he was never going to do: he'd fallen in love with JoJo. This had started out as a partnership, as two like-minded individuals who wanted to get rich and get rich the easiest ways possible. At no time had they talked about long-term or a relationship. Not in so many words. They'd simply become a couple, fooled around and fell in love.

Rick wondered if JoJo was really in love with him, though. Was she even capable of love?

He'd always assumed she felt the same way he did, but now he wondered if this was convenience or if she really felt the way he felt.

Listen to me acting like a schoolgirl, like this is some Harlequin romance or Hallmark movie. Some stupid romance, Rick thought.

He went back inside. JoJo wasn't in their room and Rick was hungry so he went downstairs to the kitchen.

There were enchiladas and flautas as well as bottled water and bottled rum on the table. Everyone else seemed to be outside by the pool, eating and acting like they were all best friends.

Rick decided he was going to take a walk and see how far he got before Cuba and his men dragged him back.

Even though Cuba had said none of them were his prisoners anymore, Rick knew better than to think Cuba was going to let him wander without supervision.

Especially after Cuba had been shot at.

Rick piled food onto a plate and grabbed two bottles of water. He wanted to have some rum but decided he needed to be focused and ready for anything.

Acting casual, Rick took a couple of bites of an enchilada as he walked to and out the front door. By the time he got to the gate, he was wearing half of the food on his shirt.

If I was smart I'd go back inside for a fork, Rick thought.

Instead, he slid the rest of the enchilada to the side of the plate and took a few bites.

There was a man with an automatic rifle near the gate, but he glanced at Rick and turned away.

Did Cuba's men have orders to ignore anyone inside the compound but then shoot them if they left? I could only get a few steps before I got a bullet in my back, Rick thought.

"Delightful weather we're having, right?" Rick walked closer to the guard and smiled. "There's food inside. You might want to get some before it's all gone."

"I ate, gringo." The man turned away from Rick, staring out the closed gate.

Rick finished another enchilada. The flautas might be easier to eat but no less messy. "Can you do me a favor and open the gate? I need to walk this food off and don't want to do it inside. A stroll to the beach might be nice."

The man turned back to Rick and frowned. "Use the door, gringo."

Rick saw where the man was looking and smiled. There was a door near the gate, so Rick walked out. He tensed up, expecting to be shot or an alarm to go off.

He started walking down the road with no real destination in mind. Simply being by himself was nice, and away from Cuba's prying eyes.

Once he got into town and had finished his food, he'd decided on a proper destination.

I'm going to see Nacho and make sure everything is back in order in his world, Rick thought.

He knew the boy would do an excellent job in finding out information about the treasure and the happenings in town, but Rick also needed Nacho to give him the information first, before it went to Cuba. That way he could manipulate it for his own cause, and hopefully keep Cuba at bay for as long as possible.

JoJo might already be on the wrong side of this, but until she told Rick she'd given up, he still felt loyal to her. He decided to keep all of this under wraps but he wouldn't completely shut her out, and hope for the best.

Rick wondered if any of this was going to play out properly, or if he'd end up dead and never knowing if there was actually a treasure, what it was, and who ended up with it.

All he could do right now was put his own plan into motion. Maybe whatever Grace had going would tie into it and be even better.

Maybe Grace is like her father and will screw me over, too, in which case she'll need to be eliminated like anyone else who gets in my way, Rick thought.

He wished he'd taken a couple more flautas with him when he'd left.

FORTY

Staying in town wasn't an option. Too many people looking for him. The only choice was the obvious one, but Baker had another problem when it came to traveling. At some point since he last used them, either the U.S. government, or the Mexican cartel had frozen his accounts.

Getting to Mexico City wouldn't be too bad. The bus, though unfortunate to have to use, was fairly cheap. Even though it would be a long, hot trip, Baker figured he would be better off in a crowd. And besides, taking a private car wasn't an option at this point. Not when he needed to raise money for a flight out of the country.

He felt like a loser, giving up on the treasure. He felt even worse going back home to his wife and not only having to explain where he'd been, but explaining it with empty pockets.

Baker figured it was better to go home with nothing, than to not go home at all. He'd find another way to help his wife. There had to be a better way.

He remembered seeing some kind of pawn shop in town. Not the ones like in the States where it was all flashing lights and big yellow signs. It was under the radar, easy to miss, but he had noticed it because of an old guitar in the window he admired.

It took him a while to find it. Eventually, once you're off the usual roads, every turn starts to look the same. At one point, Baker wondered if he was going in a circle.

He wasn't sure how much a ticket would be. He should have looked that up beforehand. But he figured it should be around the same price as the one-way ticket he'd bought to come down to Mexico initially.

Baker had sold everything in his bag that the guy would take, but still wasn't where he needed to be to feel comfortable enough to get to the airport. On the walk to find the pawn shop, he knew it might come down to the one item he hadn't had out of his sight in a couple decades.

It wasn't an easy choice but, again, it was better to get home alive and with nothing than be dead in the desert somewhere. Possibly missing limbs.

"To pawn. Not sell," Baker said as he handed over his wedding ring. Despite the slim chance of him ever making it back to this town, he wanted to leave the option open to be able to get his ring back. Hell, maybe he'd be able to pay someone in the area to get it and ship it back to him.

Yet another thing to have to explain to his ailing wife.

After making the exchange and pocketing the cash, he grabbed a drink to calm his nerves and try to forget about what he'd just done. The man at the pawn shop had given him more than he thought he would get for the ring, and Baker even counter-offered with a higher number that he had accepted. He could afford a drink or two without worrying about the price of a plane ticket.

He'd booked the trip down under a pseudonym, one of two false identities he'd spend a lot of money on a few years back. One of the couple times he was put out on the field, he'd dealt with some individuals who he didn't want to meet again. If they found out his identity and he needed to run, he had to make sure he couldn't be traced.

Nobody knew about his fake passport name but him. Funny thing was, Baker was pretty sure it had been made and sold to him somewhere around the area he currently was. Strange how that works out.

He was slightly concerned about purchasing the ticket under that same passport, but he had no other choice. If he got nabbed at the ticketing desk, then so be it. He would have done everything he could at that point.

The bus pick-up wasn't far from where he was, and as he rounded the corner he had only just begun to sweat from the sun.

The stall selling water and snacks came into view and Baker began a beeline toward it before he noticed two men stopping male passengers as they got on the bus. They weren't giving them more than a cursory look. Obviously, they knew who it was they were searching for, and knew that person wouldn't be Mexican.

Baker figured if he turned around now, he'd make himself more of a target. Kind of like whipping around and going in the other direction at a traffic stop.

He tapped the man next to him on the shoulder and gestured at his hat. He dug a ten-dollar bill out of his pocket and shook it at the guy. The man shrugged and handed over his sweat-stained, dirty Mets hat.

Baker didn't know where he would have gotten a Mets hat around these parts, but if a local had it, then it would pass. Despite the awful choice in baseball teams.

He didn't have the option to turn around, so he did the only other thing he could do in the situation. They were looking for an American. He would have to not be American.

He went off toward the refreshment stand, pretending he was going to order, then slipped to the side and got on his knees. As much as it grossed him out, he began rubbing the dirt on his face and arms. The entire time he berated himself for doing something that felt completely wrong. But he had no other choice. This may not work, but his white skin would for sure get him caught.

There wasn't a mirror to see how he looked. He assumed he appeared as if he had rolled in the dirt, which wasn't too far off from the truth.

Nobody better be taking pictures, Baker thought. *If this gets out, my career is over. If I haven't already destroyed it.*

He got back in line and shuffled with it, keeping his head down, but not making it too obvious he was trying to hide his face.

He was three people away from the bus's door when the two men grabbed someone out of the line and hauled him off to the side, yelling something in Spanish that didn't sound good.

Within a few seconds, he was on the bus and in a seat before the men let the guy go and moved back to their position by the doorway. Baker wondered if they'd noticed anybody else had gotten on the bus, and if they would board to check, but soon the doors closed and the two men walked off to the side. Presumably to wait for the next round of riders.

Baker sighed as the bus picked up speed and left sight of the checkpoint. There were long cords running each side of the bus, with fans bolted to the roof and connected to the cords in a way that made him doubt his chance of surviving if one of the electrical lines came loose.

But he was happy there was at least a breeze running through the place, no matter how hot and muggy it was.

His eyes were closed when he felt a weight push down on the empty spot next to him. He opened his eyes, remembering what he looked like and hoping whoever his seat neighbor was wouldn't beat the hell out of him.

It turned out a beating would have been preferable.

Agent George See, the current bane of Baker's existence, sat smiling at him, waving a paper fan at his face.

"You know, they told me they'd be able to stop you from getting on, but something inside me just knew you'd find a way to get around it. I didn't expect this overtly racist manner of doing it, but good for you. You're thinking on your toes. Hopefully, after we're done with you, you'll still be able to walk on them."

FORTY-ONE

Arturo couldn't even look at Catalina because of the shame.

"How are you feeling, Arturo?" Catalina asked. She'd brought him a bag of plantains, his favorite. "Your mom says you've been sleeping a lot since you got home."

Arturo thanked her quietly for the snack but put the bag off to the side. He'd eat it later, while he was cycling emotions, between anger and embarrassment.

"Has Ignacio been by yet?" Catalina asked.

"No. Why? Is he coming to try to kill me again?"

Catalina frowned. "What do you mean? He didn't do anything. He wasn't even there when the shooting happened."

Arturo shook his head. "Oh, he might not have been physically in the cafe, but he set it in motion. Don't you see, Catalina? He sent that man to kill me. Because he's scared. Weak. He knows I can do a better job than he can. Make us all more money. You'll see. The truth will come out."

"He said you messed up and took advantage, but he has no ill-will toward you. He said he still considers you a friend and he needs your help," Catalina said. "We have a new job. A big one. We'll all make lots of money, too."

Arturo shook his head. "He wants me dead. He threatened me when I was in hospital and unable to defend myself."

Catalina sighed. "When he was in hospital and weak, you took away his crew. I imagine he could have easily killed you, but he didn't."

"I could have killed him," Arturo shouted.

A second later his mother opened the door and asked if her son was alright and if he needed anything.

"I'm fine, la madre. I'm talking to Catalina."

As soon as she closed the door, Arturo sat up in bed. The wound felt raw and he could feel his blood pulsing around it, trying to escape. The pain wasn't so bad since he'd been given pills, but he knew they'd wear off soon enough. "I won't work for him."

"You're making a huge mistake," Catalina said.

"Am I? Ignacio will never trust me again, and I don't blame him. He knows I'm stronger and better than he'll ever be. He'll try to undermine anything I bring to the crew, and make me look like a fool. He's the fool, Catalina, not me." Arturo punched the air in frustration.

Catalina had been standing at the end of his bed. She took a step toward him but stopped and turned away, heading to the door.

"Where are you going?" Arturo asked.

"You're angry and not making any sense." Catalina shrugged. "I'll see you again when you calm down and are healthy. Don't try to start a war with Ignacio."

"Why not?"

Catalina stared at Arturo. "Because you will lose." She left the room before he could say another angry word to her.

In his heart, Arturo knew she was right. Ignacio might not physically be big, but he had brains and drive that Arturo knew he lacked. The right thing to do was to never see any of his former crew members again. Go on with his life as if he'd never been in the gang. As if he'd never done the things he'd done, not only to Ignacio but in general.

And what had really happened to Leo? He'd been Arturo's best friend. Confidant. They'd shared their dreams, their fears and had made a pact to get out of this town alive.

Now Leo was dead, and no one seemed to care. His name was never mentioned, and Arturo didn't even know if there had been a funeral.

His death was simply another statistic, another poor boy killed in a bad town in Mexico. Nothing more, nothing less.

Arturo turned over and buried his face in the pillow. This was all too much. He felt overwhelmed. He never wanted to get out of bed and face life again.

What if I killed myself? Would anyone care? No one would think about me ever again, Arturo thought.

His mother knocked on the door again. "Arturo, are you hungry? I can make you something."

Arturo rolled onto his back and wiped the tears away. "Yes, please and thank you."

He listened to her walking away to make him something to eat.

Arturo got up, sitting on the edge of the bed.

She would care. My mother would care about me if I killed myself and I need to remember that. I need to stop being selfish and do what needs to be done, no matter the cost. No matter the blow to my ego and my pride. I am the breadwinner in this household and I need to make us money so we can live, Arturo thought.

He'd stop being so stupid and get well. Ignacio had done a great job up to this point, and Arturo knew he'd never be able to do the things his former friend had done.

"Better to make amends and show Ignacio I can be a good soldier for him, rather than proving what a bad leader I would be," Arturo whispered.

He stood on shaky legs and walked to the kitchen, sitting down at the table.

"No, no, go back to bed. I'll bring it in," his mother was saying, standing at the stove. "You need your strength. Is it hurting again? I think it's time for another pill."

"I want to eat here, with you. I'm so bored in my room," Arturo said. "I read all of the comic books already. I want to go outside and see my friends."

His mother clicked her tongue. "Maybe in a few days. The doctor says it could get infected. You need to be careful, and I know how rough you and your friends play sometimes. Better to relax and let your friends come and see you here, like that pretty Catalina." His mother glanced at Arturo and smiled. "Is she of interest to you, son?"

Arturo groaned. "I'm not going to talk to you about my love life."

"Love life?" His mother laughed. She flipped the quesadilla she was making him in the skillet. "You're too young to have a love life."

"How old were you when you met my father?"

She frowned and stared at the food cooking. "Too young, Arturo. Much, much too young. Remember that. Nothing good can come from young love, except heartache and loss."

Arturo knew he'd hit a nerve. His mother never talked about Arturo's father, who'd left town as soon as he found out his sixteen-year old girlfriend was pregnant. His family shipped him down to Honduras, and Arturo's mother never saw him again.

She slid the quesadilla onto a plate and set it before her son.

"Aren't you going to eat, mother?"

She looked like she was about to cry. "I have no appetite. I'll make a big dinner. Rice and beans. You need to eat and then go and rest."

Arturo took a bite but he wasn't hungry anymore. He'd made his mother sad by bringing up his deadbeat father, whoever he was. Wherever he was.

No matter. Arturo was going to someday marry Catalina and they'd have children that Arturo would love. He'd never abandon his family, never make anyone sad to think about him.

First, he needed to gain his strength and go and see Ignacio, and hope the boy wasn't going to try to kill him. Again.

FORTY-TWO

Diego wasn't happy when George showed up with just Ernie.

Well, fuck Diego, he thought. *He thinks I'm working for him, when I'm using him to climb the ladder.*

Agent See sat in the car, gun pressed against the back of the passenger seat, ready to put a bullet through Baker's chest if he tried anything.

He hadn't bothered with Ernie. Sure, the guy was considered big time in the underground world, but he could barely walk, let alone try to fight off anybody. That's why he always had other people around him: to do the heavy lifting.

George wondered about that, while they drove to Diego's house.

Why hadn't there been any of Ernie's men at the hotel? He remembered reading something about Ernie's crew. Some long-time second-in-command nut-bag who went by Dominico, or Rio, or some shit like that.

Where was he in all of this?

George hadn't given it much thought until now. It was way too easy to grab Ernie than it should have been. He either had everyone out working at whatever it was he was doing down here. Or, somewhat more intriguing, there had been a falling out, and the nut-bag – Cuba, that was it – had jumped ship. Probably taken most, if not, all of the men Ernie had brought down with him.

He was also curious about how Baker, the desk jockey, had gotten tied in with Ernie. Was he playing both sides of the border, like George was? He couldn't imagine that, unless Baker was some kind of master of disguise, fooling everyone around him into thinking he was a useless twit.

Baker shifted in his seat and coughed, unsuccessful in his attempt to hide the trombone punch of a fart that came out of him.

George rolled down the window and grimaced.

That wasn't it. Nobody could be that good.

Which meant Baker, per usual, had fallen ass-backwards into some shit he couldn't handle and was not probably going to meet a cartel death because of it. George wouldn't wish that on his... actually, he'd wish that on a lot of people.

George tapped his thigh with the gun. He couldn't wait to get this over with. Hand Baker over to Diego, get his cash, and then sit on a beach nearby with an umbrella drink and plan how to screw over Diego.

It wouldn't be hard. The guy was acting without his boss's approval. If George had any family, he would have long ago learned not to take any of their killings personally. He vaguely remembered the relatives he once had. Family wasn't all it was cracked up to be.

They pulled in front of the house and he saw Baker's shoulders slump. Maybe he hadn't thought any of this was real.

Though, knowing his reputation in the agency, Baker should have known better.

"Come on. Out," George said. He motioned with the handgun and waited patiently as Baker got out.

"Really great of you to backstab another agent, See. Trying to get more brownie points from hell?"

"We're already in hell, Baker. Did you not know that? And you're about to get knocked down a few levels."

"Do you think you're ever making it back across the border after this? I'm undercover, you idiot. Deep. How do you think I got so close to Patek, and Guerrero? Once the DEA finds out about this, you're a man on the run for the rest of your life."

"Sure. Obviously. And you know that? Just the other day I shit gold bricks and built myself a new El Dorado. Save your breath, Baker. We both went through the same training. I know what you're doing, and you're not even doing it well."

"Seems to be my life lately. At least I tried, right?"

"If that's what you want to call it."

"What are you doing this for, anyway? What's in it for you?" Baker asked.

"Initially, just a reason to get away. Was supposed to bring you back. Then this Diego asshole drags me into his car and pitches me a plan with no way out. I take it. You see, I figured it was a good way to finally go underground. Once word gets back to the DEA that your body was found, it'll be obviously – and wrong – to them that this was all the cartel. They'll figure I got just as unlucky as you, but my body hasn't popped up yet. After a while, I get a posthumous burial and I'm free to do what I want."

"Are you sure that word means what you think it means?"

"Shut up," George said.

George walked him the rest of the way in, to the sunken den where Diego waited.

Ernie was on his knees, his hands tied behind his back, and his face looking like he had gone a few rounds with Tyson. He had to give it to the guy, though. There weren't any tears flowing down his face.

George grabbed Baker by the collar and rushed him down the three steps to the den floor, tossing him next to Patek.

"There you are. Two meatheads, as promised."

"Thank you, Agent See," Diego said. George noticed the blood on his knuckles. He admired a man who did his own dirty work.

"Since I don't seem to be in need anymore around here, I'll be grabbing my payout and heading off to a long vacation."

Diego nodded and gestured at one of the men in the room. The guy walked out and George listened to his footsteps fade.

"Any suggestions on some nice beaches where I can get drunk and watch a bunch of big asses walk by?"

Diego lit a cigar, poured himself a drink, and flicked at the ice cubes as he approached George.

"Oh sure, there are mucho places like that around here. The Atlantic side is just as tantalizing as well. But you know where you really should go if you want some strong drinks and thick women? A little town just outside of Rio. Cleaner beaches. Not crowded. Except for the asses, of course."

George waited impatiently for his money to arrive so he didn't have to listen to this Mexican douchebag. He was envisioning how Diego would die when he heard the name of the town he was talking about.

"You ever been there?" Diego asked.

"I've been to a lot of places. It gets hard to keep track."

"Oh, I think you'd remember this one. Lots of beautiful women. In fact, there was one woman there. Prettier than the rest. Had a little child. He had his mother's eyes. He had my eyes, as well. They say children tend to take after one or the other parent, but this boy, well, he was equally a mix of both." Diego put his cigar down. "You understand, Agent See, that even if these two weren't involved with the death of my brother, I still would have picked you up at that airport. Except it would have gone very differently. But what better way than to have the man who killed my wife and child bring me the men who killed my brother?"

George knew better than to hear Diego out any further. He raised his gun, but only got halfway up before a boom sounded behind him.

He saw the front of his chest explode before he collapsed to the floor and everything, including his dreams of the future, faded.

FORTY-THREE

Rick didn't approach Nacho's house, instead hanging down the street on the corner. He knew Nacho had his crew watching right now, but he didn't want to let them all know he was here.

He trusted Nacho but not the rest of them. Besides the fact they'd turned their backs on him so quickly for Arturo, Rick knew any of them could also be working for the cartel and tip them off to his whereabouts. Rick was exposed not being in the villa with Cuba, his men and their weapons.

Better to take his time and assess the situation. He remembered some of his FBI training from a long time ago, and knew he needed to stay focused and ready for anything.

One thing Rick had learned so far in life was to be prepared for the things you could never prepare for.

He decided to circle the block and come in from the rear, sure there was a way without being seen. The streets were packed with people but no one seemed to be watching him, and he didn't see any children or teens hanging out in strategic spots, either.

Maybe Nacho wasn't even home right now. He could be out somewhere, looking for the treasure. Had they even made the deal before Arturo was shot? Rick knew Nacho was going to dive right in and search. Rick also knew the kid had a good shot of finding it, better than their many diving excursions, and Nacho might run off with it.

That would be a kick in the ass, to have Nacho end up with the treasure and the rest of them broke, Rick thought.

Of course, if anyone besides him or JoJo was going to get it, he supposed Nacho would be the next on his list he'd be happy for.

The back of the building looked clear, but Rick knew prying eyes could be in every window. He casually strolled up and down the block first to make sure there was no one hiding. Sure it was safe, at least in this moment, Rick slipped through a backdoor to the building.

He heard the sounds of families behind the flimsy doors but knew where he was going.

No one stopped him. Rick knocked on the door and a moment later Nacho's mother opened it a crack.

Was she his mother, or was Maria, though? It was so confusing, like Grace with Ernie and Cuba. Didn't anyone know who their real parents were anymore? Of course, I wish I had had different parents, Rick thought.

"Is he here? I need to talk to him," Rick said.

She didn't look happy but she opened the door and let Rick inside. The smell of her cooking made his mouth water.

"Would you like me to make you one of my special quesadillas, sir?" The woman still didn't look happy, but Rick saw a gleam in her eyes.

"I couldn't ask you to do that, ma'am... but that does smell delicious," Rick said and smiled.

"Ignacio is in his room. Give me five minutes and I'll make you some food." She scurried off into the kitchen and Rick went to Nacho's door and knocked.

Nacho didn't look surprised when he opened the door and waved Rick inside, looking past him. "Are you alone?"

"Yes, and hopefully we won't get interrupted again, although your mother said she was making me a quesadilla." Rick went to the window and looked down, expecting to see Cuba and his armed men pulling up. He decided to stay at the window while they spoke, at least until the food was ready.

"I think I have a problem. Actually, I have a couple of them, but one is bothering me right at the moment," Nacho said.

Rick shrugged. "Then we focus on one at a time. Tell me what's on your mind." He had a vague idea of what he wanted to talk to Nacho about, so figured he'd be the nice guy and let the kid vent for a few minutes, maybe get an answer for his problem, and they could refocus on the important things right now.

"Arturo. I sent Catalina to talk to him, to feel him out, but I think he's going to come for me. I can feel it. He's not only been demoted but his takeover didn't work like he thought it would." Nacho shook his head. "I need advice. Do I be the bigger person and ignore it, hoping he comes to his senses and realizes he can't lead this crew like I can... or do I do something I might regret someday?"

Rick wanted to tell Nacho to grow up and stop worrying about the little things, but this very well might turn into a bigger thing. If Arturo was making waves and making trouble, it could hurt finding the treasure.

"Ever killed someone?" Rick asked jokingly.

When he saw the pained look on Nacho's face he frowned and put up his hands.

"Wait... you have? How old are you? When did this happen? Does anyone else know? Who did you kill?" Rick put a hand over his mouth because he was babbling and Nacho looked like he was ready to bolt.

There was a knock at the door and his mother came in with two plates and enough quesadillas for a dozen hungry people.

"Thank you. Gracias," Rick said and took both plates and put them down, nodding to the woman until she left.

Nacho had acted casual, but as soon as his mother closed the door he threw himself down on the bed and buried his face in his pillow.

"Forget I even asked, Nacho. Let's eat and we can figure it all out."

Nacho lifted his head, wiping the tears. "You eat. I already ate so much. She cooks too much. I'm going to be fat."

Rick didn't like the way Nacho was looking at his gut. Rick turned away and took a plate with him to the window, where he began eating and trying to hide his belly from the kid.

"I killed Leo," Nacho said, sitting up on his bed. "He deserved it. Arturo deserves to die, too. I have these awful thoughts. Do you ever have evil thoughts like that, Mister Rick?"

"All the time, kid." Rick took another bite. The food was delicious. *Of course, I don't always act on those evil thoughts. I usually control the desire, even if I want someone to die*, Rick thought.

"Do you ever act on the impulse to kill?" Nacho asked.

Rick sighed. He waved the food in his hand. "You're making me not enjoy this, Nacho. Yes, I have killed people. Not only bad guys the FBI told me to kill, either. People I knew. People who could get me in trouble and someone I was relatively close to. That was a long time ago, but it still haunts me."

"I don't want to be haunted for the rest of my life." Nacho looked like he was going to cry again.

Rick didn't know the right thing to say. He'd come here to make sure the kid was going to help look for the treasure, not thinking of killing another kid. This was going to be bad and distracting at a time when Rick needed Nacho to be focused.

"You give Arturo the benefit of the doubt. Let him make the first move or look like he's going to. Then you pounce and make sure he doesn't get the actual chance to take you down," Rick said. "The key is to always keep him close to you. Never let him go off on his own."

"Why keep him close, if it could be easier for him to kill me?"

Rick smiled. "Keep your friends close and your enemies closer."

Nacho nodded. "Sun Tzu."

"Nah. That's from the second *Godfather*, kid. You need to watch better movies."

FORTY-FOUR

Grace watched Rick leave the property. It was strange. Alberto had to basically beg Cuba to let him go to the boat. The rest of them didn't even try to leave. Was Cuba actually holding them here, or was he relying on them thinking they were captives? That way later he could claim he never forced any of them to stay?

She was pretty sure JoJo would have a more difficult time getting out from Cuba's sight. Alberto made sense to want to keep around since he was the captain of their boat. Grace thought she may be able to just walk away without any issues, but had no plan to as long as the treasure was still on option. Cuba probably knew that.

No, Rick got out so easily because Cuba didn't have a need for him, other than not harming him to keep JoJo happy. It was the same reason why Rick wasn't shark food after shooting Cuba with the flare gun. Killing Rick would mean killing any chance of having JoJo for himself.

Grace figured he could kill Rick and just force JoJo to be with him, but Cuba wasn't that type of guy. He wanted the woman to make the decision to stay not by coercion, but because they found him irresistible. It was an ego thing.

All she really knew for sure was that Rick was out of the plan. He was a loose cannon at this point, and Grace learned a long time ago that if someone wasn't one-hundred-percent then they shouldn't be involved in anything important.

She would have to figure out how to move forward with just herself and Alberto. Not impossible, but not easy.

They were supposed to go on another dive in the morning. As much as Grace would like to not tag along, to lay out by the pool and enjoy a rare moment of silence, she would have to. Despite her refusing to do anything while on the dives, she knew that as long as she kept showing up, Cuba would think that she was interested in helping. That would keep some suspicions off her.

She wondered if Rick would be there. If he would even come back before they left. He might be done with everything at this point. Grace figured she'd find out in the morning.

She wandered into the library, her favorite place besides the pool to relax.

"Oh, sorry. I'll leave you alone," she said as she walked in and saw JoJo sitting in one of the recliners.

"No, come over. Please. We need to talk."

"I told you, there is no plan."

"Not about that. At least, not yet. You know, I've been doing this long enough to know when something is up. You remind me of myself at your age. Smart, cunning, attractive. You know enough to get most anything you want from people, but not enough to know how to survive."

"You'd be surprised at what I know."

"Arrogant, too. That'll go away as you start making mistakes. Hopefully you'll learn from them."

Grace sat at the chair across from JoJo after grabbing a drink. She figured at some point she'd have to get this conversation over with. JoJo didn't seem to be the type to let things go, no matter how much you told her no.

Moments like these, when best laid plans were tossed aside, you had to improvise. The part Grace thought would be a problem took shorter than expected. She had to give Alberto credit. The man had connections. Which meant he could also be dangerous. He didn't appear to be the type to double-cross, but she wouldn't put it past anybody. Especially not with the supposed amount of money the treasure would provide.

Life-changing, never have to worry about anything again, tell people to fuck off type of money.

Grace just didn't want to bring JoJo into it. She'd say it was nothing personal, and she wouldn't exactly be lying. She didn't know her enough for anything to be personal. She just didn't like the bitch and had no desire to help her.

Let Cuba take her. They'd probably do well together.

"What do you know about the metamorphosis?" Grace asked.

"Like Kafka?"

"No, like Houdini."

"Nothing at all. I hate magic."

"Well, a little bit of misdirection may get us away from Cuba, with the treasure." Grace refilled her drink. She motioned at JoJo, who nodded, and poured a second glass. "See, Houdini had this illusion in his act. He'd have himself tied up. Ropes, handcuffs, the usual. They'd lock him in a wooden trunk and his assistant would take a sheet, cover herself for a moment, and when it was whisked away, Houdini was standing in her place. When he opened the trunk, she would be inside, tied up."

"Great story. Yawn. What's the point?"

"I'm trying to tell you something without really telling you something."

JoJo rolled her eyes. "Kids today. Can't just get to the point."

"Do you want a part of this or not? I'm not even sure I really want you in on the idea, but your shitty, bitchy attitude isn't helping. Angry you're getting old and losing your looks? Don't take it out on me."

JoJo leaned back and sipped her drink. Grace noticed the 'old' comment really got to her. She'd have to remember that for the next time she started giving her shit.

"I apologize. If you haven't noticed, I haven't been having the best of times in this situation. Feels like my entire life has been spun around." JoJo looked at Grace. "You don't want me involved because you think I'm too close to your father, right?"

"You're not far off. And don't call him my father."

"It's not what you think it is. Yes, I'm pissed at Rick, and I probably will be for a while after this is all over. And did I think of maybe leaving him for Cuba? There were a few times. I mean, the guy is easy on the eyes, and built like a... anyway. But I don't want that. I don't know what I want, but I know once this treasure is found I don't want to see Cuba anymore."

"But a part of you feels like he's full of shit? Like after you help him get the treasure he'll leave everyone dead in the water and take off?"

"Why do you think I keep coming to you? We need a way out of this that doesn't involve us being dead."

"Funny you should say that."

"What do you mean?"

"I'll let you know later. For now, you got about as much out of me as you will. I still need to think on it."

"A story? That's all I get?"

"Sometimes a story holds a lot more to it than you'd think. Sometimes it's almost exactly what you think it is."

JoJo shook her head and stood. She finished her drink and began to walk away and stopped, turning back to Grace.

"The Houdini thing. You're going to switch out the treasure?"

"Close, but no. Don't worry about that for now. Get some sleep. And when Rick gets back, try to talk some sense into him so he doesn't get us killed before we have a chance at the treasure."

FORTY-FIVE

Rick simply walked past the guard and back to the kitchen for a snack, even though he'd eaten well at Nacho's house thanks to his mother. Or aunt. Whatever she actually was.

He was supposed to meet with Nacho either later tonight or tomorrow, depending on what Nacho was able to dig up. The boy had seemed preoccupied, and Rick knew that wasn't good.

Nacho killed that other boy. I would've never guessed he had it in him, Rick thought.

Not that he thought any less of Nacho. In fact, the kid had a set of brass balls, especially at his age.

If Nacho eventually killed Arturo, Rick would not be surprised. More surprised if he let the other boy live longer than he was useful.

Rick wondered at what point Cuba was going to deem Rick no longer useful. It would definitely be sooner than later. Cuba might only be keeping Rick around because of all the unknowns in their future.

Who am I kidding? He's keeping me around so he could look good in front of JoJo and win her over, Rick thought.

Rick found a bottle of coconut rum and two glasses, filling them with ice. If he couldn't find JoJo he'd drink from both glasses and get a good buzz.

There were too many thoughts swimming in Rick's head, and he went to the pool to relax for a bit.

He was alone, which was nice. He'd figured Grace would be out here getting a tan in a skimpy bikini. Glad she wasn't going to distract him, and sad about it as well, Rick poured both drinks. If JoJo was around she'd see him and come to investigate. If not... he had a bottle of coconut rum to empty.

Rick had set up a lounge chair so he got the full brunt of the sun, which also let him see into the villa on the far side of the pool.

He saw Cuba walking toward him, but when Cuba noticed Rick he frowned and spun on his heels and went the other way.

Good. I don't feel like answering your dumb questions and being bothered, Rick thought.

The rum was delicious. He'd eaten more than enough to know it might take the entire bottle to get drunk, which was fine with him.

Nacho might come calling tonight, and he'd need to have some of his senses sober.

There was something else on Nacho's mind, but Rick couldn't figure out what it could be. Nacho looked like he wanted to say something important today, but Rick knew not to force it out of the kid. He'd get to it in his own good time, and maybe that was why he'd insisted they meet again so soon.

Nacho might have a few leads already, or he might even know there was no treasure. He had his ear on the flow and ebb of the town, and maybe this was simply a rumor that had been started years ago. The cartel might have started it, or likely had also heard it but had never acted until now.

Rick took another sip and shook his head. It could literally be anything at this point. No use in wasting the rest of the day trying to figure out what Nacho was going to tell him.

He knew it was going to be something significant. Rick could feel it. Either because of his FBI training, his survival skills or his ego. Whatever the case, he'd find out. Hopefully tonight.

Grace came outside, wearing only a skimpy red bikini. "For me?" She came over to Rick and picked up the second glass with the melting ice.

Rick smiled and gave her a generous pour of coconut rum. "How's it going?"

"Fuck off," Grace said and walked away.

Rick stared at her tight ass as she swished it back and forth, disappearing inside.

"I had an ass like that, a long time ago. You should've seen it. It was amazing. You could bounce a quarter off of my ass-cheeks," JoJo said from the balcony above.

Rick hadn't seen her step outside, too busy paying attention to Grace's ass.

"You still have a great ass," Rick said and smiled. "I had a second glass for you, but the little girl took it with her."

"I'll get another one and be right down. Need more ice?"

Rick nodded.

In a couple of minutes, JoJo joined him near the pool and they filled their two glasses.

Rick held his glass up. "A toast."

"To?"

"How about to us?" Rick asked.

JoJo shook her head and clanked her glass to his. "Here's to swimming with bow-legged women."

They both laughed.

"Where'd you go today?" JoJo asked after taking a sip of her drink. "It looked like you walked right out the gate."

Rick smiled. "I did. Cuba said we weren't prisoners so I found out if it was true. I guess it was. He didn't bother to follow me as far as I know, unless my evading skills were rusty."

"No, he was here. Bothering me for a bit. Nothing too important. I think he's getting bored with you, though, Rick. Bored isn't the right word."

"He wants me out of the picture so he can have you," Rick said. He decided the rum was good and hitting the right spot of his brain and he didn't want to go the subtle route. They might as well have a real conversation about them. About JoJo and Cuba. About the future.

JoJo shook her head. "And I don't get a say in who I want to be with? Does that sound like me?"

Rick put up a hand. "Hey, I'm just calling it like I see it. You do still have a great ass. That's all I'm saying. Cuba is definitely noticing and wondering what you're like in the sack." He might not be subtle but he'd never ask her flat-out if Cuba had already gotten to sleep with her. If she said no he might think she was lying, and if she told him they had... Rick thought that might just crush him, more than anything in his miserable life.

Jojo shrugged, which was probably the worst thing she could do to Rick. He wondered if she'd done it on purpose, showing him she wasn't going to talk about any of this unless she wanted to. JoJo led the narration, and she knew it.

"Thanks for the drink," JoJo said. She finished the rum and took the glass inside with her.

Rick watched her ass swish as she moved, and smiled. He knew JoJo was doing it because Grace had done it.

For an older broad, you still got it, Rick thought. He wondered if he could make a move on her tonight, if Nacho didn't appear. It had been far too long since they'd been intimate.

"Way too long," Rick mumbled into his freshly poured glass of coconut rum.

He was definitely going to finish this bottle, get sunburned and take a long nap by the pool.

FORTY-SIX

Ernie's face felt like he'd been run over by a steamroller, fixed up, then beaten to death by a gorilla.

And still he couldn't help thinking that he hadn't eaten since before him and Maria went out to find Cuba.

While they were beating him, nobody told him exactly why they were doing it. Sure, that now-dead DEA agent said something about this Diego guy thinking he'd killed Raul. But Ernie had been in the game long enough to know the full story was never out until the man in charge sat with him.

Which he had done right before Baker was dragged inside and tossed next to him.

Ernie now had to wait even longer, still in pain and still hungry, while Diego's men killed the agent – good riddance – and things settled down.

"Where have you been?" Ernie asked once Baker got his face out of the carpet.

"Trying to get out of town. I just made it out of the hotel. Had to take down a couple guys. No big deal. I am a trained DEA agent, after all. What happened to you? I saw them drag you out all soaked."

"Boat went boom."

"And Maria?"

"Alive or dead. Depends on Cuba's mood."

"How'd you let her get captured? Weren't you both armed?"

"First of all, Cuba had a couple men with bigger guns. Second, I gave her over. Thought I could trade her in for my daughter. Apparently, Grace didn't want to come with me."

"What did they grab you for anyway? Agent See has no issue with you. Or, I guess, he *had* no issue with you," Baker asked as he swiped away a piece of George from his shoulder.

"They think we killed Raul. This dude coming back over was his brother. So we're here because the brother of one of the heads of this area's cartel was murdered and we're getting pinned for it."

"Not a good situation."

"Not a good situation." Ernie agreed and faced Diego, who had sat back down and re-lit his cigar.

Diego watched them for a while, saying nothing, while his men took the dead body out of the room. Ernie made enough eye contact to show a bit of confidence, but not enough to come off as cocky. The way Diego looked at them was scary enough to make him not want to look at him at all.

"So," he finally said, putting his cigar in the ashtray, "Ernie Patek and... you, the guy with the weird name."

"It's a family thing," Baker said. Ernie jabbed him in the ribs. He didn't need to get shot before he got to plead his case.

"Great. Good to know. Anyway, here we are. I'm looking at the two men who killed my brother. We got a good beating in on you, Ernie. Maybe we should make Baker look like your twin before we get down to any conversation."

"Didn't do it." Ernie winced, more from the idiocy of his replay than the pain talking made.

"Oh, I know that," Diego said. He snapped his fingers at someone behind them and was brought a drink a minute later.

"You know what? That we didn't kill your brother?" Ernie asked.

"You catch on quick."

"But... but what the hell did you beat the shit out of me for if you knew I didn't do it?"

"Because it was fun. Who wouldn't want to have some one-on-one time with Ernie Patek. You're a hated man in this country. Good for getting things done, but a pompous asshole."

Great. They broke his face for no reason. He had no leg to stand on when it came to convince Diego of their innocence because he already knew they had nothing to do with Raul. Ernie would have thought they were as good as dead, but there had to be some motive behind going through all the trouble to bring them here.

"So we're all friends then? Gonna give me an ice pack, a couple tacos, and a car to get back to town?"

"I like carne asada," Baker said. Ernie elbowed him in the ribs again.

"Not right now. You see, I do need you two for something. Though, I guess I really don't need both of you. We'll deal with that later. I told Agent See a little white lie in order to get him to bring you both here. To keep my name out of any problems that may have arrived from grabbing two Americans in the middle of the day. As I told him before his heart flew halfway across the room, my main reason was to get him in here and kill him."

Diego gestured at another man behind them and pointed to Ernie and Baker.

Ernie flinched as he felt hands grab him and lift him up. Keys rattled and the handcuffs around his wrists dropped to the ground.

"Please, have a seat."

Ernie and Baker sat. He felt a moment of anger at the fact that he got his face beat in and Baker got off easy.

"What is it that you want from us?"

"I know Maria Guerrero killed Raul. Not only because there were multiple witnesses, but because she never tried to hide the fact that she hated Raul. She hated him even more when he was moved up to be right underneath her."

"Good to know, but, again, what do you want from us?"

"Same thing I wanted from Agent See. I want you to bring Maria to me. We thought she might be with you, but nobody found her in the hotel. Which means she either escaped, or was out doing something else. Since the three of you were seen together coming back to town, I would assume you know where to find her. Or, at least, how to get that information."

"Cuba has her," Baker said.

"What would Castro want with Maria? When was she taken?"

"No. Cuba was my second-in-command. He recently defected. He somehow got a hold of Maria and took her away. It was a shame when I heard of it," Ernie said. He was certain Diego wouldn't like that he'd handed her over.

"Do you know where this Cuba is?"

"I do know. I've known where he's been ever since he backstabbed me and stole my daughter."

"And how is that?"

"My daughter. Grace. I bought her a pair of earrings a few years ago that she wouldn't stop begging me for. She wears them constantly. I made sure to have a tracker installed in one of them in case something like this would happen. I didn't think one of my own men would take her, but I figured it was a matter of time before someone used her for leverage against me."

"Good. So you will bring me Maria, whatever it takes, and then we'll be even."

"And what's to say you don't do to us like you did to the guy with the hole in his chest?"

"Just like life, there are no guarantees. My men will escort you out, and you will get that car. As for the tacos, you're on your own."

FORTY-SEVEN

Cuba didn't trust Maria and wondered if he trusted JoJo, Grace or Rick.

The old days were so much better, when I followed Ernie around and got his scraps. When I made more than enough money and got more than enough women because Ernie was too stupid and arrogant to see what I really was, Cuba thought.

Especially when it came to Ernie's wife and the long affair they'd had.

Tomorrow he was going to try another few spots to dive at, but Cuba was worried. If he was underwater, whoever was left on the boat might speed away and leave him. They could also tamper with his scuba gear and kill him. They might have a truce right now, but Cuba knew it wasn't real. Once the treasure was found he'd begin taking them out, and he knew they'd be ready.

If he stayed on the boat and let JoJo, Rick and Grace dive, he worried they might find the treasure and not tell him. Slip away later and grab it and run.

Maria was also going to be a problem, since he couldn't trust her to dive. He didn't even know if she was capable of it, either. He doubted she'd had instruction. Maria would need to stay on the boat, which meant someone would need to watch her at all times.

Then there was Alberto, who was too quiet for Cuba's liking. The man was more than capable of piloting the boat, but he was also more than capable of somehow hurting Cuba.

If Maria told Alberto to speed away or he'd face the wrath of the cartel, Alberto might feel he had no choice. With Cuba, Rick, JoJo and/or Grace searching below, it would be the perfect opportunity for Maria to make her move.

Unless I leave her at the villa, Cuba thought.

He couldn't bring all of his men with him anyway. Better to lock Maria inside her room and have a guard posted at the door and one below so she couldn't escape.

Cuba needed to hit the ground running tomorrow. At this point, he hadn't even come close to finding the treasure. He didn't even know if it existed. Maybe Ernie had been lying, playing another one of his games. He wouldn't put it past Ernie because he'd done some weird long-term grifts in the past.

He remembered the time Ernie had tried to buy a small South American country with a fake offshore account, or the time he'd claimed to have found the Holy Grail in the mountains of Tibet and raised half a million dollars from investors to recover it.

There was no Holy Grail in Tibet as far as Cuba knew.

Ernie did these things not because of the money but because of the rush of doing them to begin with. Ernie Patek was a true wild card, latching onto something obscure or unknown and trying his best to find it or possess it.

Even when it isn't real, like this treasure might be, Cuba thought.

The smart play for Cuba right now would be to cut bait and run. He had enough money to live relatively comfortably for the rest of his life. He could figure out how to drain a couple of Ernie's accounts without the man even knowing. What was keeping him in Mexico right now?

Surely not the elusive idea of a treasure. It likely didn't even exist.

Cuba shook his head. He knew why he was still in this mess.

Because I am also like Ernie Patek, Cuba thought. The thrill of the chase is more important than the kill. The idea that there could be something at the end of this is exciting. Titillating.

He also knew he wanted to see what happened with JoJo, and if she was going to be with him. It was a definite egotistical move, but Cuba had lived his life being steered by his ego. Not a big deal and nothing too against the grain of what he usually did.

There was also Grace to consider. Could he have an actual relationship with his daughter, his flesh and blood? She was a handful. He'd watched her grow up into the spoiled, cliche rich brat she was.

Grace was also cunning and perhaps more focused than Ernie was, which also made her infinitely dangerous. No man, including either of the men who were considered her father, would be able to tame her and her drive.

Three more diving days and then I will need to reassess, Cuba thought.

If three days passed and there was no treasure or even a hint of one, then he might need to leave. Not tell anyone, either. Simply get in his SUV with his team and drive to the airport, hire a private jet and go... where? Cuba had nowhere to actually go now that he'd crossed Ernie Patek.

The houses, the resorts, the mansions, were all in Ernie's name. Cuba was sure by now Patek had spread the word that Cuba couldn't be trusted, and he might have even given the order to shoot on sight. No, Cuba would need to take his money and find a new, remote location.

Somewhere off the grid, but not too far from civilization. As much as he was enjoying the sea and the sun of Mexico, he didn't want to live in a country like this. He could go back to Puerto Rico, but the thought of returning to that wretched place made him sick.

No, he would need to find a safe haven far, far away.

Perhaps Norway or Sweden. He'd never been but he knew Ernie had no pull in either of those countries. It might be the perfect landing spot for Cuba, and his money should go far.

The uncomfortable question still remained, though: could he, should he, leave without having JoJo and/or Grace with him?

Both women could easily walk away from him, or simply watch Cuba leave and continue the search for the treasure.

The treasure does not exist. I'm sure of it, Cuba thought.

But he'd search for three more days. Without any real location in mind, he'd ask Alberto what he thought. What his feelings were. It might give Alberto the false sense of thinking he was part of the team and not just the boat driver. As if he would get an equal share of the treasure if it was found.

Cuba knew if he left the country he'd still need to keep track of them, because in the rare chance they did find the treasure, he'd need to come back for it. Need to take it for himself.

Why am I doing all the hard work, when it would be easier to leave a man here to watch them, and then swoop in when it was time? If there was no treasure or it was never found, then Cuba had paid someone to keep an eye on JoJo and Grace. Still worth the price.

Maybe then I can reach out to one or both of them and reconnect, Cuba thought. *Have them rendezvous with me in Norway or wherever I was living.*

Cuba had no use for Rick or Maria, or even Alberto. If it came down to it and he saw an opportunity, he decided to kill Rick and Maria before he left.

You both have three days to live, Cuba thought, picturing both Rick and Maria dead with a bullet wound right between their eyes.

It would be a nice going away present to himself. Then JoJo could eventually get over Rick's death and be more receptive to being with him.

Maria dying would just be a bonus, because he did not like the woman. He wanted nothing to do with her or the cartel, and if anyone was going to find a treasure it would be the combination of JoJo, Grace and Alberto. Maybe even Ernie and Baker would swing back around to help.

Then Cuba could kill the rest of them too, leaving only Grace and JoJo. Maybe Alberto if he gave up his share of wealth and stepped away, to live another day.

Cuba decided to get something to eat and then do some research on Norway or Sweden on his phone before bed.

The morning was only a few hours away, and he'd need sleep if he wanted to have the strength for a few more dives in the next three days.

He frowned when he saw Rick walk out the front door. Where was he going this late at night? It didn't matter.

Cuba hoped Rick got caught by the cartel or was leaving, which would only help Cuba.

FORTY-EIGHT

Alberto was in bed, trying to sleep when the door opened and the light came on. Grace stood in the doorway. If he didn't know better, he'd assume this was some kind of late-night booty call. But Grace wouldn't have any interest in him. Only in porn would that happen.

He sat up, rubbing his eyes, pretending like she'd woken him from a deep sleep.

"What's going on?" he asked.

Grace shut the door and slumped down in the chair by the bed.

"We have to bring JoJo in, I think. She's been bugging me and she's not stupid enough to believe nothing is going on."

"I don't know if that's smart. The way Cuba is always hanging around her."

"It could be a good thing. I don't like her, but she's useful. And I think Cuba makes it seem like she's more into him than she is."

"She seemed pretty pissed at Rick. Why not hook up with Cuba? You bring her in, you run the risk of everything you say getting back to him."

"No, she's a bitch, but she's not crazy enough to get involved with him. And besides, who says I need to tell her everything? You don't know everything. And I can seed some fake shit in there so if she does talk to someone about it, I know it was her."

Alberto didn't like that he wasn't filled in on everything. If he had the full picture, he could help with coming up with alternative ideas if needed. He felt like a pawn at the moment. Both with Cuba and Grace. Weird to have father and daughter tugging at him from both ends.

He needed to decide what he really wanted. Not what everyone else thought was best. If there was ever a time to look out for himself, it was now.

Even though initially Cuba had seemed to have them locked in like prisoners when they weren't out diving, he'd seen Rick walk right off the property a little while ago. Maybe it was Grace who was the actual villain here. She was looking to take the treasure from her father and would do anything, and say anything, to accomplish her goal.

Sure, Cuba was an asshole, a killer, a sociopath, and who knew what else. But he didn't seem to be treating them as anything worse than temporary players in his hunt. Maybe he really did plan to cut them all in and let them go their separate ways at the end.

Grace seemed to want to take it all, and the less people involved, the better.

He would have to think on this for a bit. She may not have told him everything, but he knew enough and had set up enough so far to be able to derail the plan up to the last minute. If it came to that, Alberto wouldn't hesitate.

"Fine. Tell her what you want. Does she need to know I'm involved? I'd rather keep that secret."

"I'm pretty sure she knows already, but there's no reason to bring it up. But when the time comes, we'll all need to work together if we have a chance of pulling this off."

"Is that doubt that I hear?"

"Doubt? Me? Never. It's more like... being cautiously optimistic."

Grace left and Alberto watched her go.

If only I was twenty years younger, he thought.

Alberto wouldn't have let himself get into this situation when he was younger. But, he did do a lot of other dumb things without the prodding of someone else. Giving that up and going legit – kind of – was probably why he was alive to witness that ass walking away.

He waited for the creaking of Grace's footsteps to go away before getting out of bed and slipping on a pair of sweatpants. There was no way he was going to sleep anytime soon after that conversation, and he knew better than to try to force it.

He walked past the other bedrooms. Light came from under JoJo's door. The same with Grace. Cuba's room was on the other side of the house, an area he'd never been to. Alberto doubted Cuba was in there yet. The man seemed to be up at all hours and ran on no sleep. If he didn't get at least eight hours in, he was almost useless the next day.

As far as he knew those were all the bedrooms. He wondered where they'd put Maria. Was there a basement here? She might be shackled up in chains, naked, being forced to eat like a dog.

I really need to get laid. God, he thought.

He walked past the kitchen, heading to the library and a large glass of tequila on the rocks.

"Wait," Cuba shouted from inside the kitchen. "Come here."

Alberto knew he was still up, but he was hoping they wouldn't cross paths. Though he was stupid to walk past the kitchen, the one place in the house that Cuba liked to hold court in.

He backtracked and walked into the room.

Cuba was sitting at the large island, his big arms propping himself up. An almost empty bottle of scotch was next to him and, from the look in his eyes, all the rest of the alcohol was in his stomach.

"Sit. Sit." Cuba gestured to an open chair. "Go back to your posts. Let me know when Rick comes back," he said to the two guards.

This was either going to be a short talk about tomorrow morning, or a very long talk about anything that popped up in Cuba's saturated brain. Maybe he should look at the situation in a more positive light. Cuba droning on and on would be the best sleeping aid he could get.

"What did you do the other day?" Cuba asked.

"When?"

"When I let you out to do your check on the boat."

"Pretty much what you said. I checked the boat."

"Pretty much, huh? Yeah, you pretty much checked your boat and then you pretty much headed to the beach bar and talked with some man. According to my guy, it was longer than just a hello."

"You had me followed?"

"Of course I had you followed. I need my captain going off to the authorities or, worse, the cartel? Or maybe being stupid and trying to sail away? What did you two speak about?"

"Just chit-chat, you know. We're old friends. I hadn't seen him in a while."

Cuba typed something into his phone and poured the remaining scotch into his glass.

"That is all? You are sure?"

"Yes, that's all. I figured since I was out, why not grab a beer without being surrounded by gunmen? I happened to see him there and sat for a bit, then came back."

"You know my men went up to him after you left. Had a chit-chat, as you say, with him as well."

Alberto shifted in his seat, trying to make it look like he was adjusting himself instead of beginning to feel really nervous.

"So what did he say? I'm sure the same thing as me."

"He said a lot. Unfortunately, almost every word out of his mouth was gibberish. The man was too drunk to speak. It was a shame. But that's okay. I'll send my man out again to find him when he's sober. Which, from the description, is almost never. So if you have anything to add, do it now."

Alberto shrugged. "Chit-chat."

Cuba smirked and dismissed him.

He'd have to have another talk with Grace. If what he set up is compromised, and Cuba didn't have them killed, they'd need to come up with something new.

Despite his hopes, he'd be getting no sleep tonight.

FORTY-NINE

Ignacio had given the signal to Rick that they needed to talk tonight, but he'd worried Rick hadn't seen the three quick flashes from outside the walls of the villa.

When he saw Rick casually strolling toward the gate, Ignacio had relaxed. Just a little. This could be a setup, or maybe the others inside were all watching to see where Rick was headed before they sent out a few men to follow.

He wasn't completely sure he could trust Rick, or anyone else for that matter.

Life was hard when you had to watch your back all day and all night.

Ignacio knew he needed to find a safe spot for them to talk, and he knew just the one.

Rick was following, half a block back, being careful, which made Ignacio happy. It meant he'd snuck out and no one likely knew he was gone. If they could meet and talk quickly, Rick might be able to sneak back inside.

When Ignacio got to the beach he made sure there was no one lurking about and no one walking on the sand.

He waited for Rick to arrive, trying to figure out what he was going to tell Rick. How much information he needed to give to the man.

Can I trust Rick? I think I can, Ignacio thought.

"Hey, Nacho. I hope this means you have something for me, because if they catch me sneaking out at night they'll know something is up. I don't trust Cuba at all right now, and I think he's going to attempt to kill me soon, to be honest," Rick said.

Ignacio nodded. "I have some information for you. For Cuba, but you know what I mean."

"Did you actually make a deal with Cuba? I don't think you actually spoke with him." Rick kept looking around. "Where is your crew?"

"Arturo made the deal for the crew. I'm now leading them again, which means I take on the contract. I will go to him in the morning and let him know what I have found, unless you want me to hold off for a day or two." Ignacio had his hand out. "And are willing to pay for my silence for a time."

Rick chuckled. "I always enjoy working with you, Nacho."

Ignacio waited until Rick took out his wallet and handed over two crisp twenty dollar bills.

"The cartel has Ernie Patek and Baker Cioffi. So far they are both still alive," Ignacio said. "They are looking for my aunt, Maria. I don't know why but it is not so they can throw her a party. She has either done something to hurt the cartel or they think she has. I cannot find real information, although I have heard some rumors about a betrayal."

"I'm listening." Rick sat down on the sand and Ignacio followed. If anyone was walking through the thick canopy of trees or on the beach they might not see the pair now.

"Two DEA agents have been found. Dead. Not sure who killed them but the cartel doesn't seem too happy, because that might bring down the full force of your government. They don't want the Americans in Mexico getting in their way of doing things," Ignacio said.

Rick frowned. "Were the DEA agents already working in the area, or are they new?"

"Both of them are new. They flew into Mexico City and drove here from what we gathered. Also there is a third DEA agent in town, and he was the one who captured Ernie Patek and Baker Cioffi and delivered them to the cartel," Ignacio said.

"Ugh. A rogue agent on the cartel payroll. I knew it wouldn't be a surprise if we uncovered one, but still... that can't be good for us finding the treasure." Rick stared at Ignacio. "What else?"

"That's it so far," Ignacio said and looked toward the ocean.

"Tell me what else you know, Nacho. So far all of this is good and Cuba will pay you handsomely for it, but I know you're holding something from me. Spill it." Rick stood and offered a hand for Ignacio to also rise.

"There is something but I don't know if I should share it with you," Ignacio said. He stood and paced around the beach in a tight circle. "Can I trust you, Mister Rick?"

Rick shrugged. "As much as you can trust anyone, I guess. Look, Nacho, we're on the same side. We want the same things. We're moving forward together in all of this. Have I ever screwed you over or tried to hurt you?"

"No. You have not." Ignacio knew if he told Rick about what he was thinking, this would change everything. For all of them. He was still undecided over how to proceed.

"Do you know something about the treasure?" Rick asked.

Ignacio nodded slowly, staring into the darkness, his eyes slowly adjusting to see the faint line where the sky met the ocean in the distance.

He'd been born here and this town was all he knew. He might not know every local, but he knew enough of them. They all knew him, they all traded favors and information and pesos, and there was a definite limited trust. As long as Ignacio and his crew didn't upset the balance or go against the locals, everything would be good. For everyone.

Rick was an outsider. He might upset the delicate balance.

He also might get me out of this town and let me see the world, Ignacio thought.

"I want to leave this town. Leave Mexico. See other parts of the world. See not only the United States but spend a winter in Canada, a summer in Italy and a month in Australia." Ignacio turned to Rick and smiled. "I want to grow older and stronger and kiss pretty women in Japan and Germany and Florida."

Rick chuckled. "Don't we all, Nacho."

Ignacio shook his head. "No, this is not a dream. What you might call a fantasy. This is what I want to do and I want you to promise me you will help me to make it happen. Once I show you what I have. Do we have a deal?" He put his hand out for Rick to shake.

Rick stared at the hand and smiled. "What are you up to, Nacho?"

"Ignacio. My name is Ignacio."

"Fine, kid. I'll try to remember that. Nacho sounds better, like a personal inside joke you and I have together," Rick said.

Ignacio still had his hand out. "We are partners if you shake, which means you cannot screw me over. You cannot take what is mine right now. Do we have an understanding?"

Rick frowned. "Wait... what do you have, kid?"

"I have what you have been looking for," Ignacio said.

"Show me." Rick started to look around again.

Ignacio wondered if Rick thought he was being set up or if this was some ploy from Ignacio.

"I won't show you until you make a promise to me you will not screw me over," Ignacio said and reached further with his hand.

"Fine. I can live with that." Rick shook the boy's hand. "Now, what is it you're being so cryptic about?"

"Do you have a flashlight on you?" Ignacio asked.

When Rick pulled one from his pocket, Ignacio took it but cupped the light with his hand and only moved his fingers every few steps toward the water's edge.

"Where are you going?" Rick asked, catching up.

Ignacio walked into the waves and kept using the light for a second or two so he knew where he was headed. The water was higher than the last time he'd been out here, but he knew the treasure chest might still be seen.

"There," Ignacio said.

"Holy shit, Nacho... are you kidding me?" Rick laughed when he saw the top of the chest sticking out of the water. "It's right there. This entire time. We're out there diving and wasting time, and you have it. I'll be damned."

"We are partners," Ignacio said to Rick. "There are several underwater. I have not been able to open them or dig them out. We need to work together."

Rick scooped up Ignacio and hugged the boy.

FIFTY

Grace waited for Alberto to go back to his room, then slipped on a pair of sneakers and walked out the front door.

The stars were shining in the clear sky, and the sound of waves in the distance soothed her. A light breeze ran across her exposed skin. The temperature had dropped to below burn your face off level.

She walked down the driveway to the dirt road that led into town. A guard stepped out in front of her and held his hand out.

"Go back inside."

"Why? I'm going for a walk. Back off."

"Cuba said nobody leaves."

"Bullshit. I watched Rick just stroll out of here. If he can go whenever he wants, then Cuba's fucking daughter can also. Back off. That's the second time. You won't want to be your nut-sack if I have to say it again."

The guard held a finger up to her and turned his back, taking his phone out. Grace could have eavesdropped on the call, but she didn't need to. Obviously, the guard was checking with Cuba, not wanting to get his junk smashed.

After a minute, he hung up and moved to the side, gesturing for her to go. As she passed, he grabbed her arm. It took a lot of effort for her not to break his wrist.

"Rick can go out because he's useless now. Cuba said to be back in half an hour or we come find you."

Grace glared at him before moving on.

Cuba's idiot guards couldn't stop her from taking a walk. Half of them she'd tasered when she made her first escape. They were all incompetent.

She thought about that escape and smiled. It was one of her better moments. She was still proud of assembling that homemade taser. It's a shame she couldn't keep it.

Not that it mattered, really. It had done its job, which wasn't just to aid in her escape. But to make Cuba want to keep her around. To bring her on the dives. To make sure he had eyes on her the entire time so she wouldn't get away again. Little did he know, she had no plans to run away again.

It was only a quarter mile to where she was heading, and she could have gotten there in almost no time, but Grace walked leisurely. She was enjoying the sound of the seagulls and the smell of salt water.

Despite being out on a boat all day for the last however long they'd been searching for the treasure, she'd never get tired of the ocean. She was more comfortable on the water than anywhere else.

In the distance, lit by the moonlight, what looked like a man and his kid walked the beach toward the water. Probably just dipping their toes in. They had no idea how close they were to the house and what went on inside. To them, it was just another clear night to enjoy.

Grace turned a corner, then walked off the road into the vegetation. It wasn't as dense here as some other places, and she made her way through with only a couple scratches. The bug bites were the most annoying part of the trip.

A little bit into the woods, enough so that a passing car or person wouldn't be able to see, she came to a clearing. It looked man made, with obvious machete marks on the chopped down plants. It was only now, after thinking of a machete, that Grace thought about snakes and if she should have taken better precautions going into the jungle.

There were no snakes, but Grace wasn't alone in the clearing.

Two men stood there, shadowed by the canopy. They didn't exude danger as much as... hunger.

"Hey, Dad," Grace said.

"Come here." Ernie gestured with his hands and Grace embraced him.

"Any problem getting out of the house?" Baker asked.

"Nothing I couldn't handle. I gotta get back soon, though. By the way, next time you give me earrings I don't care if they have a tracking chip in them, but let me know that you can hear and talk to me through them as well. Scared the shit out of me when you first said something. Good thing I was alone. And I now know to put these far away when I'm in certain... situations."

"It was for your protection, not for me to spy on you. I figured it was a matter of time before someone tried to grab you and extort me. Never thought it would be Cuba."

"Well, he did have sex with Mom. That should have been your first hint."

Ernie shrugged. "Can't change the past, right?"

"No, but we can change the future by getting this treasure and taking care of Cuba. I don't care who he is to me, the asshole's got to go."

"Great acting on the boat, by the way. He really thought you meant it when you said you wanted to stay with him. And the plan we talked about? How is that going?"

"First off, I'm a great actor. After this, you should pull some strings and get me some juicy Hollywood parts. Second, the plan is going fine. A hitch with Rick, who seems only focused on trying to repair his relationship with JoJo. Alberto's still on board. He set up getting the other boat. I just need to let him know when."

"I'll let you know. Make sure you keep your earrings in, though. I still need to hear everything and let you know how to proceed."

The three of them stood there in silence for a while. Baker kept slapping at his arms and neck, obviously wanting to get out of the area and away from the bugs.

Grace didn't know what else to say. It didn't matter, though. She could get a hold of her father at any time.

Cuba thought Ernie was an idiot. He'd never think they were in constant contact since he took her from the boat and killed her boyfriend. While she was smart and capable, she wasn't yet ready to go out on her own, and appreciated the help when she needed it.

"I'm bringing JoJo on. I just haven't told her yet."

"I know. I heard the talk you had with Alberto on the way here. He brings up good points."

"Do you think I'm doing the right thing?"

"Of course you are. You pick up on things quick. Just like me. Better than me. Bring JoJo on. If Alberto knew what was really going on, he wouldn't care. Then again, he'd be pretty pissed."

"Leading him down a path to a fake plan, just to find out later he had no idea what the real plan was? Anybody would be pissed. But we still cut him in, like we agreed. He's a good guy. Could be useful in the future."

"Agreed. And JoJo?"

"I couldn't care less about that bitch. Let her rot."

By the time Grace got back to the house and into her room, she was smiling. Luckily, Cuba hadn't seen her, since a rare smile on her face would make him suspicious.

Fuck him, Grace thought. *Even if he did get suspicious, he'd never be able to figure out what was really going on.*

Grace shut off the light and got under the covers.

Tomorrow would be another long day on the ocean. And the next day. And the one after that, until she was ready to take Cuba and his entire crew down. Until then, it was fun in the sun and a lot of day drinking. You couldn't beat that.

"Goodnight, Daddy," Grace said, before taking off her earrings, putting them on the nightstand, and drifting off to sleep, a smile still on her face.

About the Author

Armand Rosamilia is a New Jersey boy currently living in sunny Florida, where he write when he's not sleeping. He's happily married to a woman who helps his career and is supportive, which is all he ever wanted in life...

He's written over 200 stories that are currently available, including crime thrillers, supernatural thrillers, horror, zombies, contemporary fiction, nonfiction and more. His goal is to write a good story and not worry about genre labels.

He also loves to talk in third person ... because he's really that cool.

ABOUT THE AUTHOR

Born the same week Animal House was released, Tom Duffy has been on Double Secret Probation ever since. ABBA was also on the top 10 music charts, and Andy Gibb was Shadow Dancing at #1. The author has no problem with any of these things.

Printed in Great Britain
by Amazon